BURNT ISLAND

ALICE THOMPSON WAS born and brought up in Edinburgh. She was the keyboard player with post-punk eighties band The Woodentops and joint winner, with Graham Swift, of the James Tait Black Memorial Prize for Fiction for her first novel, *Justine*. Her second novel, *Pandora's Box*, was shortlisted for the Stakis Prize for Scottish Writer of the Year. Her other novels are *Pharos*, *The Falconer* and, most recently, *The Existential Detective*. Alice Thompson is Lecturer in Creative Writing at Edinburgh University.

ALICE
THOMPSON
BURNT
ISLAND

SALT

CROMER

PUBLISHED BY SALT PUBLISHING
12 Norwich Road, Cromer, Norfolk NR27 0AX United Kingdom

© Alice Thompson, 2013

The right of Alice Thompson to be identified as the author of this
work has been asserted by her in accordance with Section 77 of the
Copyright, Designs and Patents Act 1988.

First published by Salt Publishing, 2013

Printed in Great Britain by Clays Ltd, St Ives plc

Typeset in Paperback 9.5/14.5

ISBN 978 1 907773 48 8 paperback

1 3 5 7 9 8 6 4 2

To Nick Royle

'THEN THINK WHAT would happen to them if they were released from their bonds and cured of their delusions. Suppose one of them were let loose, and suddenly compelled to stand up and turn his head and look and walk towards the fire; all actions would be painful and he would be too dazzled to see properly the objects of which he used to see the shadows. So if he was told that what he used to see was mere illusion and that he was now nearer reality and seeing more correctly, because he was turned towards objects that were more real, and if on top of that he were compelled to say what each of the passing objects was when it was pointed out to him, don't you think he would be at a loss, and think that what he used to see was more real than the objects now being pointed out to him?'

Republic
PLATO

PROLOGUE

'I feel like I'm on an island,' he told Dr Hoffman.

'What kind of island?'

'Rocky. Angular. Cypress trees like black, sinuous totems of death.'

'The island represents a kind of death wish?'

'A living death wish. A perpetual sense of living doom.'

'That you try and shake off with ambitious dreams for your career?'

Max looked at Dr Hoffman with the utmost respect. Where were these ideas coming from? She had seemed so superficial in her cream trouser suit and blonde ponytail and now she was making so much profound sense.

'But you say you keep seeing this other Max?'

'That is correct.'

'Doppelgängers are omens of death.'

'I didn't know that.'

'Where do you see him?'

'Standing in the dark shade of the cypress trees.'

'What did you feel when you first saw him?'

'Incredulous. Curious.'

'Do you ever chase him? Try to catch him?'

'By the time I realise it's me, he's gone.'

'I see.'

She wrote all this down in her childish loopy handwriting. It was like Sylvia Plath's handwriting, he thought. All this pain written in such schoolgirl matter-of-fact handwriting. The only thing missing was a smiley face for the dot of the 'i' in suicide.

'Well, it's been an interesting session,' she said.

'Any suggestions, Dr Hoffman, any suggestions?'

She gave a wry laugh, as if the last thing any self-respecting psychotherapist would do would be to make a suggestion.

'I would suggest you write it down. Whenever you see a doppelgänger write it down. There's scientific proof that writing things down can ease stress by 50 per cent.'

'But can writing ease doppelgängers?'

'I should think writing could do a lot of things to doppelgängers. Not least make them less scary and more understandable.'

'I never told Dot about them.'

'Of course not. She'd never have understood.'

And she gave such an intimate sly smile of understanding it turned him to stone. It was as if she had known everything before and everything he'd said had simply been confirming what she already knew. She had not been writing down what he was saying but just going through *the motions. He had the overwhelming, eerie feeling that she already had a book written of his life in a cupboard somewhere, written in her childish, loopy handwriting, documenting everything.*

CHAPTER 1

THE SEA WAS darkening, as if a malevolent spirit had entered its depths and taken on the form of the shifting, rising black water. Streams of white foam spumed from the burgeoning waves. Peering through the storm's heavy mist for a sign of the island, Max clung onto the wet railings of the passenger deck as the small ferry lurched from side to side. A huge wave suddenly rose up over the side of the boat in a wall of solid, angry ocean, and splashed down over the deck, soaking Max's face and clothes in deathly-cold water before sliding back into the sea.

'Quite a gale,' Max ventured to shout over to the dour ferryman, through the wind and rain, his face dripping with icy water.

'Indeed it is,' the ferryman said. He was standing at the prow of the boat, staring like Captain Ahab over the stormy sea, wearing an expression of inscrutable triumph.

'I imagine storms are quite common over here,' Max said, looking for reassurance.

'Never seen one as bad as this before,' the ferryman replied.

Max tried to remain calm, taking deep breaths from his abdomen as his therapist had advised him to do in stressful situations. The boat veered suddenly to port and his suitcase, which had been propped up behind the railings, slowly slid over the side like a coffin in a sea-burial. Max clutched tightly onto his sodden hold-all, which contained his pens and notebook, as he watched his suitcase slip swiftly and succinctly beneath the waves.

The ferryman, who had watched silently as the whole thing unfolded, turned around to him again.

'Had you not stored it properly?' the ferryman asked.

'If I had stored it properly,' he shouted back over the wind, 'it would not have gone over the side.'

'True enough,' the ferryman said, a rictus smile breaking out. 'It's always best to store things properly.'

Max's anger at having lost his suitcase was being trumped by his growing fury with the ferryman. Why did people insist on stating the obvious? One day soon, he thought, he would state the obvious. He would state the obvious in his next book.

Once the sea had swallowed up his suitcase, the storm abated. His shirts and underpants and home-knitted cable jumper had clearly appeased the wind gods. Burnt Island was now appearing out of the mist, a huge, black rock rising inevitably from the sea. A flock of dark birds suddenly flew out from the gloomy interior of a large cave on the edge of the coastline.

'Does that cave have a name?' Max asked.

'Prometheus' cave,' the ferryman replied. 'After Prometheus.'

Prometheus, who was chained to a rock and had his liver eaten by a vulture for all eternity – rather like being a writer, Max thought. The ferryman moored at the little pier at the bottom of the cliff and Max leapt onto dry land with the relief and excitement he always felt when stepping onto solid ground.

A steep path, hewn into the dark rock, rose precipitously up the cliff face. Max looked down to see the ferry making its way back to the mainland, a tiny dot in the great expanse of black sea. A makeshift handrail of a chain hanging between rusty metal poles was all there was to separate Max and his hold-all from a hundred-foot drop onto rocks and waves. As he climbed the steps, he hung onto the loops of the chain so fiercely their rust ground into his palms. In spite of himself, he imagined his body leaning over the handrail as far as it could go and then falling to its death.

He finally reached the top of the cliff. There were a few hundred yards of flat grass dotted with sea clover but no sign of habitation at all. For a moment he wondered if he had been the victim of a cruel hoax, which the benefactor and the ferryman had both been in on. There was nothing on Burnt Island. It had all been burnt. A seagull hovered above him. In the early summer dusk he felt strangely elated. He could just die here alone, he thought, unmourned, his next novel unwritten, his disappearance perhaps doing wonders for his previous book sales.

The sea was now flat and still beneath him. The sun was setting over the horizon, staining the sky crimson and gold. Sunsets made him feel nostalgic for Dot and Luke. He was never quite sure why. He supposed it was the sunset's mixture of the sublime and the ephemeral. One moment, sunsets were the most transcendent thing in the world, the next they had gone. He lay down on the grass. Considering he was on a rock dotted with periwinkle, in the middle of the Atlantic, it was bizarrely warm. His clothes, still damp from the sea, were gradually drying out.

He shut his eyes. *He had to think of a plot.* He was putting all his trust in Burnt Island by coming here. Burnt Island would produce a story for him, perhaps even, if he were lucky, some characters. His plan for his next book was for the plot to stick out like the spokes of a wheel. It would work in a circular motion, all its intricacies clearly on show.

He fell asleep. When he woke up it was dark. He was shivering. This was ridiculous, he thought. There was nothing like being surrounded by nature to remind him of how vulnerable he was. What could he do? He didn't want to wander around in the pitch darkness. Just then he saw a small light moving about a few yards in front of him. It was the beam of a torch.

'Are you Mr Long?' came a voice out of the darkness.

Max nodded and smiled, hugely relieved.

'We were worried about you. Your boat was due in three hours ago. Where did you moor?'

Max pointed to the pier.

'The ferryman must have decided to come in on this side of the island because of the wind.'

'Then I fell asleep,' Max explained.

There was silence.

'I was tired,' he continued.

'I'm Peter. I'm to look after you on the island.'

Peter was standing only a foot away from him and Max could now see his lugubrious face quite clearly. He was in his thirties, with dark hair and vivid blue eyes. He had a heavy bone structure but a slightly scared-looking face as if Max had done him some wrong a few years ago and he'd never forgotten it. *Stop making things up,* Max thought to himself.

'Well, thanks for coming to look for me in the dark. I might have walked over a cliff. But I didn't. As you can see for yourself . . .' he trailed off.

'I'll take you to your croft. It's not far,' Peter said.

They walked together in the dark, only the narrow line of grass in front of them illuminated by the torch beam. The ground grew rockier and they seemed to be walking upwards. Bats scattered in wild formations above their heads. They finally arrived at a croft with two small windows on either side of a decrepit-looking door and Peter took a key from under a stone on the windowsill and handed it to him.

'It's not locked,' Peter said.

'Why the key then?'

'I was told to give it to you.'

'Are you employed by the benefactor of the fellow-ship?'

'Something like that.'

Peter shook his hand. 'I live next door to the garage, where I work.'

'Right,' Max said.

Peter turned, and Max watched as the beam of his torch disappeared over the other side of the hill.

He pushed open the door. It stuck. Max gave a kick and it opened with a feeble squeak. He climbed a small step into the gloomy bothy. The floor moved unsteadily under his feet as he staggered around in the darkness, bumping into various objects inside the room before locating a torch on the mantelpiece. As he picked it up, he knocked a small china ornament off the mantelpiece, which hit the floor with a crash. He swore under his breath, as he shone the torch around the interior.

It was a small bothy, a kitchen on one side of the room and a single bed on the other. A table sat in the middle with a box of matches on it. A paraffin lamp hung out of the wall. The place was bleak and impoverished. Max was used to the luxuries of the city. He wasn't used to physical hardship. Emotional pain, yes, but not feeling uncomfortable. He would stay the night here and then find somewhere more comfortable on the island, a small hotel perhaps. One with electricity.

Rain began pattering on the small windows and the tin roof with a clattering sound. There was a general pervasive smell of damp. He took off his coat and shoes, brushed his teeth in the sink – just turning on the tap caused a terrible clanking sound and the water tasted of iron (or was it lead?) – and clambered under the single coarse bed-blanket fully clothed. He remembered with a pang the clean smell of Dot's laundered sheets: citrus. There was no way he could write his novel here. A misery memoir perhaps, but not his next novel. He tossed in his narrow bed, as he listened to the rain. He was sure the walls were shaking in the wind.

As he lay there trying to get to sleep, he recalled the advert in the *Times*: 'Fellowship for writer on island. Three months. Board and lodgings and expenses. Box 352.' He had sent a letter and copies of his novels to Box 352 and got a reply by return of post, which was, in Max's experience, very unusual.

'Dear Mr Max,' the letter began. *'I am unable to say who the benefactor of this award is, as he wishes to remain anonymous, but he greatly enjoyed the seven published novels that you sent him and also your recent novel, which in his humble opinion suffered a huge injustice in its failure to find a publisher. He has had many applicants but he feels you, above all, would appreciate these three months in which to write. You are given absolute liberty to write what you like without other duties. He strongly believes in the absolute unfettered imagination of the writer. The only thing he would ask of this totally new work is that in some way Burnt Island, as your place of residence, would be an inspiration for it.'*

~

The next morning, Max woke up to the sound of birds singing furiously outside the window. He brushed his teeth in the metallic water, feeling slightly more cheerful, but the house was even more unprepossessing in natural light. He ate some chocolate, a bruised apple and a carton of juice from his hold-all, and had a shave. He packed his few belongings back into his hold-all, put it over his shoulder and ventured outside.

Standing in front of the bothy in broad daylight, he could see to his surprise it was not stone but pebble-dash. And there seemed to be an actual gap between the building and the ground. He bent down and looked underneath. He could see *wheels*. His bothy was, in reality, a pebbledashed caravan.

A small village was nestling at the bottom of the hill. He walked down to its few higgledy piggledy streets, past a pub and a small library, until he reached the garage that consisted of a pump and a few broken carcasses of cars scattered about in front of a small, wooden shed. Max noticed a pair of boots sticking out from underneath one of the cars. He wondered what a garage was doing on an island where no cars were allowed.

He knocked and entered the shed. A single light-bulb lit up a tiny room. Sheets of paper overflowed the desk in the corner. A man was sitting behind the desk. He was better built than Max, who tended to stoop. His broad body was encased neatly in a shiny white T-shirt and jeans and his fair hair was swept back from his resilient, stubbled face. He was muscular, probably from working on the hypothetical cars on Burnt Island. He had a tattoo of a rose on his upper arm. Its silver-grey thorns were delineated very sharply and the rose petals painted a savage red. He was reading a celebrity magazine.

'Yeah?' he said in a deep voice, without looking up.

Max absorbed people like a sponge and intuitively sensed his arrogance. He knew there was a special part of the brain for self-awareness that some people had and others hadn't. He felt this virile young man lacked self-awareness. But then again, perhaps he didn't need it.

'Do you know where Peter Samson is? I was told he works here.'

The young man finally looked up.

'He does. He's my boss.'

'Was that him under the car?'

He nodded. '*Peter*,' he shouted.

A few moments later Peter strolled into the shed covered in grime. He saw Max and smiled.

'Did you have a good night in Windy Cottage?' Peter asked.

Max took out the key from his pocket and put it in the man's blackened hand.

Peter looked down at it.

'It's a caravan,' Max said softly. 'Pebbledashed. It moves in the wind.'

'You want something more stable?' Peter asked.

'Yes.'

'You'll be lucky to find anything stable on Burnt Island, won't he, Peter?' the muscular man asked.

'You should know, Ryan.'

Both men laughed.

'Lodgings will do,' Max said.

Peter thought. 'I'll see what I can do. I just thought you'd prefer something self-contained. So you could write . . . Do you have any special requirements?'

'Besides it not moving?' Max asked.

'Yes.'

'Not really. I suppose quiet. No children.'

That afternoon, Max made a quick exploration of the village and noticed everything was in very good condition. All seemed new, woodwork in pristine condition, roofs expertly slated. It was like everything had just been painted. He wondered who owned the island. He felt in some way that Burnt Island was going to be his salvation as well as a place where he could begin his next book.

CHAPTER 2

ON THE WEST side of the island there were shallow, pale-sand beaches and turquoise seas, and on the other side vertiginous cliffs dropping into the stormy sea below: huge interfaces of nature. Towers of sculpted rock stood like totems to the sea gods a few metres out from the rocky shore. There was an invariable mysticism about an island, Max thought. He couldn't help but feel islands were inviolate; they had their own special locus.

The sky was eternally dramatic; the sun appeared apocalyptic behind a coastline of jagged black rocks. The desolate, astounding beauty made him think of the end of the world. And he loved it, for the end of the world was where he wanted to be.

He explored the dunes on the west side of the island. He found the texture of dunes sensual; the combination of sharp grass and soft sand, the undulations of the ground and the flat areas strewn with daisies and sea pink flowers. He sat down in the dunes and took out his blank notebook. Out of the corner of his eye, he noticed a seagull hovering over his head. How to construct a sympathetic character, he mused? A protagonist with enough character flaws to make him seem human? The blank page stared up at him reproachfully, as if Max had hurt it, done it some damage by not writing on it. Max stared at the page. He stared at it hard.

The same seagull was still flying above his head, now flying unnecessarily close – he could almost feel the brush of its powerful wings against his scalp. The bird flew directly at him, squawking loudly and Max instinctively ducked. 'Hey!' he shouted. The bird dive-bombed him again, a huge dirty brown seagull crying out at him with a loud honking sound. He was imagining things; this wasn't *The Birds*. Max put his arms up to protect his face, too late, as the gull's beak struck his head.

He leapt to his feet, picking up his hold-all, his empty notebook falling onto the sand, and he started to run. But he could still hear the seagull's cries above him and he looked up to see the bird just a few feet above his head. *The bird was chasing him*. A newspaper headline flashed through his mind: *Forgotten and Cruelly Neglected Literary Author Pecked to Death by Seagull on Remote Island*. No, it would be much pithier than that. *Island Writer Attacked by*

Killer Bird. Or perhaps *Killer Bird Strikes* (*Again?* Has it killed before?).

More gulls were congregating above his head, their squawking growing louder. He found himself lowering his head again. Suddenly another one dived at him, close to his right ear. He ducked and, as soon as he did so, a third flew at him, shrieking, pecking at his scalp as if he were food, drawing blood. In a flurry of feathered wings and sharp beaks, they were crowding around his face. Max fell to his knees. Just as he thought he was going to be mauled to death, the birds suddenly scattered upwards into the sky.

He remained on his knees for a moment, breathing from his abdomen and brushing the sand off his clothes. A young girl was approaching and in spite of her small stature seemed to be the reason for the seagulls flying away. She had an odd, secretive aura about her. The girl bent over him and gently stroked his face, and when she withdrew her hand he saw to his shock her fingers were covered in blood: his blood.

'Thanks,' he said. 'I think you scared them away.' She gave a smile and shrugged her shoulders as if it was something she did everyday.

'Do they attack like that often?'

She shook her head.

'I must have gone near their nesting ground. I won't take it personally,' he said, but she nodded her head vigorously, as if he were to do exactly that, and turned and walked away.

Max wiped what he thought was sweat from his brow, but his palm came away stained red. He was still bleeding. Walking briskly back to the village, he passed a couple of elderly women in the street, who, with their silvery grey hair and heavy dark skirts, looked doughty. They gazed at him suspiciously and sternly at the same time.

'Can you tell me where the doctor is?' Max asked.

'What's the matter? Have you been in a fight? I know who that would be,' the taller woman said darkly.

'No, no,' he said, wondering wildly who she was referring to. 'It wasn't a man. It was a seagull.'

Instead of laughing, she said, 'Oh, the skuas. Violent creatures. You need a walking stick. I always hold it above me and they attack my stick, thinking it's my head.'

'I'll remember that for next time. In the meantime, can you tell me where the doctor is?'

'Next to the garage.'

Everything seemed to be next to the garage, he thought. He ran down the street and just next to the garage spotted an ordinary-looking, solid Victorian house with a gold metal plaque fixed above the door-bell with the name *Doctor Macdonald* engraved on it. The name seemed reassuring – the name of a highly experienced doctor on the brink of retirement, who wore tweeds. Max opened the door and entered the empty reception room. On the table sat a small bell with a label stuck to it saying: *'Ring for attention.'* If only he could ring for attention in real life, he thought. He rang the bell.

'Come in,' came a gruff voice from behind an impos-ing panelled door. He entered a large room, holding his hand beneath his chin with a handkerchief to stop the blood dripping onto the beige carpet. A middle-aged woman was sitting behind a desk, wearing glasses, her long lanky brown hair falling messily around her face. She had a mousey, grumpy, blue-stocking look as if she hadn't seen the sun in a while.

The blood was beginning to seep through the hand-kerchief, the material unable to staunch it. Max tried to look unconcerned. He would rather be bleeding to death than look like he was making a fuss. But even little fears, like appearing indecisive or looking like he was making a mountain out of a molehill, seemed to seize him on a regular basis. It was strange how often one's worst fears came true, death being a case in point.

She was still sitting immobile behind her desk, as if waiting for *him* to do something. Nowadays, Max had noticed, doctors tended not to offer a diagnosis themselves. Rather they asked him what *he* thought was wrong with him, which rather defeated the purpose of all those years of medical training. He wasn't going to the doctor for *his own* opinion. He could have given that to himself, in the privacy of his own home.

'I'm bleeding,' he finally said.

'I can see that. A seagull?'

He nodded.

'Ah, they can be dangerous around here. Especially the skuas.'

'I am worried the wound might get infected,' he explained.

'Beaks of birds tend to be very clean. Especially the seagulls. It's the saline water.'

Was she bluffing? Max wondered. He didn't know enough about saline water to be sure.

'You mean the sea?' he asked, tentatively.

'You're the writer, aren't you?'

It was funny how each person said that in a different way. Dr Macdonald said it as if it were a medical condition. How right she was.

'Yes.'

'But to put your mind at ease . . .' she relented. Soaking some cotton wool in disinfectant, she came around the desk to where he was sitting. The smell of TCP swamped him. For a moment, a brief moment, he felt comforted, her maternal closeness reassuring him. And then, the terrible pain.

'This might sting a little,' she said, too late. He bit his lip and she carefully and expertly dabbed all over his scalp. Was it his imagination, or was her dabbing just a little too deft, a little too hard? Was there some pent-up anger or even some sexual sadism in those dabbings? After a few excruciating minutes, she had finished. He felt he had never known such pain since his agent, on reading his recent manuscript, had asked him where the rest of it was.

She brought out a bandage and, parting his hair with her black-painted fingernails, carefully taped a section of dressing two inches by two inches onto his scalp. In a lot of blue-stockinged women, Max had observed over the years, some expression of the *id* had to come out – in the doctor's case, the painting of her fingernails black. He wondered if her toenails were painted black, too.

And here were her black nails applying tape to the dressing. The tape not cut with scissors but sliced in half by her small, pearly-white teeth. Was her mouth any more hygienic than a seagull's, he wondered? Afterwards, lounging almost postcoitally back in her chair, her hair falling suggestively over her eyes, she asked, 'So what do you write?'

'Well, I used to write literary novels.'

Her languid, dark eyes suddenly burned.

'You're not Max Long? *The* Max Long.' He nodded, not sure what she was going to say next. 'I love your novels. Especially the last one. The ending was unforgettable – so ambiguous. I've read all your books.'

She hesitated, staring at him suspiciously, even disbelievingly, and then asked, 'Would you mind terribly signing them?'

'Not at all.'

She jumped up from her desk and left the room. Obviously, the whole house belonged to her, the front room reserved for her surgery. A few moments later she returned, bearing a pile of seven books like the charred bones of a ritual sacrifice.

He opened one up at the flyleaf. 'Shall I write, "*To Dr Macdonald*"?'

She smiled. 'No, just sign your name.'

And he did, all seven times.

Coming out of the surgery, a large dressing plastered to his head, Max felt unaccountably joyous.

'Max!' he heard someone shout from behind him.

He looked around. It was Peter, his withdrawn, white, lantern face in its usual impassive state even while shouting Max's name down the street.

'Hi!' Max felt strangely relieved to see him. Peter seemed quite straightforward compared to everyone else here.

'I've found you a place to stay.'

Peter led him off the main road up into the dunes. They walked for a mile, twisting and turning through the prickly grass and soft sand. A huge modernist house built almost entirely of glass rose out of the dunes, overlooking the Atlantic. This was better than a caravan, Max thought triumphantly, and he felt pleased with himself that he had requested better accommodation.

'This is where the reclusive author Mr Fairfax lives,' Peter explained.

A mixture of panic and exhilaration passed through Max.

'Not the author of *Lifeblood*?' he stammered.

Peter nodded.

Fairfax, the Fairfax who had sold over a million copies a year of his first and only novel *Lifeblood*, who resisted all publicity outside the small circles of the literary world and its festivals. No photo of him had ever appeared in a newspaper or magazine. They shared the Meerkat, though.

Their literary agent, dubbed 'the Meerkat' because of his deceptively cute face and pointed chin, was a short and rotund man with a huge appetite for women and food. Each wife he married was younger and prettier and smaller than the last, like Russian dolls. The Meerkat, however, grew increasingly large, his weight just adding gravitas to his international persona. He propelled his heavy body expertly around, as if he were a Roman *testudo*.

In spite of the Meerkat's amiable face, Max was slightly frightened of him. Whenever he brought his agent a book, he felt a bit like Squirrel Nutkin bringing a beetle wrapped in a dock leaf as a present for Old Brown Owl.

Max remembered how frustrated his agent had been by his failure to persuade James Fairfax to do a European publicity tour. When Max hadn't even been able to get a book signing in his local bookstore.

'This obsession with his privacy,' his agent had muttered, ' I don't understand it. People would die for the publicity he gets. *Die*.'

Max had just looked at him. 'It's a paradox,' Max had said. 'A writer wanting attention. And not wanting it at the same time.' And now here he was, standing outside this modernist structure of glass and steel, about to enter the house of James Fairfax.

As Peter was turning to leave, Max noticed an anxious expression on his face. 'Look, if there's anything I can ever do for you, if you need help in anyway . . .' Peter suddenly said.

'Thanks very much,' Max replied, puzzled, 'but I don't think that will be likely.'

'You never know,' Peter said.

Fairfax, *the* Fairfax. What a coincidence, Max thought, as he entered the huge atrium that gaped open and upwards like the interior of a church.

CHAPTER 3

PERSIAN CARPETS WERE scattered over the open-plan living room's amber floor. Soft, white sofas and armchairs stood in the centre. The view through the massive window faced west over the sea and the sun setting over the horizon flooded the room, casting a pink hue over the white furniture like slanting sunlight on snow.

He looked up to see a man of about sixty peering over a mezzanine balcony. The first thing that struck Max, from where he was standing below, was Fairfax's energy. It came flowing down over the balcony in a tidal wave. 'Come on up. The stairs are to your right.' The voice had the resonant throbbing of a primitive machine's engine. Max climbed the steep, metal, circular staircase that wound up to the balcony, trying not to look down. The balcony was lined with bookcases, which blocked out the view of the sea. He had never seen so many books before, except in a library.

James came bounding over to him, beaming, and shook Max's hand vigorously. He didn't seem

like a writerly recluse at all. He was easily over six
feet tall, well built, with wide shoulders and a waft
of grey hair that had seemed to settle on his head
like an afterthought. He had a handsome, open face
marked by bushy eyebrows and a sensual mouth.
His eyes were an azure blue, the whites of his eyes
clear. He was wearing a soft suit of green velvet, a
creased, light-pink, open-necked shirt and brown,
laced-up shoes.

He looked more like an actor than a writer, Max
thought. He didn't seem like the publicity-shy author
of *Lifeblood*. This man was – he struggled for the word
– well, so *urbane*.

'You are Max,' James announced.

Max didn't know what to say to this incontrovert-
ible fact.

'I hear you need a place to write your next opus.'

'I do indeed,' Max replied, cursing his inbuilt tendency to mimic the tone and rhythm of the person
speaking to him. Dot said it was because he didn't have
a personality of his own. And she was probably right.
Perhaps character anyway was just an accumulation
of habits built up over the years, with a few memories
thrown in, to add to the illusion of being a real person.
But in any case, Dot had finally left whatever character he had. Like a shadow leaving the house, with a

smaller shadow holding her hand, who just happened to be his son.

'Let me get you a drink and we can discuss it,' James was saying.

Max came away from the bookshelves, reluctantly. 'Don't worry, you'll be able to browse all you want later,' James said, noticing Max's lingering look at the books.

The two men went back down the stairs to the open-plan living room. A bar stood at one end.

'Gin and tonic?' James asked. Max nodded – it was his favourite drink, although it had a tendency to make him grumpy.

James sat down on the armchair opposite him and nonchalantly crossed his legs. Max felt himself slowly sinking into the plush sofa and was wondering how he was going to extricate himself from it afterwards. Purple zigzags decorated James's socks.

'When I realised who you were,' Max said, 'I admit I was surprised. Inviting me into your home like this.'

'Well, as you know, Max, I value my privacy hugely. And us writers are some of the most self-centred creatures on the planet. And I am no exception. I'm not necessarily taking you in out of the kindness of my heart.'

Max took a large swig of his G&T. He had taken

umbrage at James's generalisation about writers but resisted the urge to contradict him. James was, after all, offering him a five-star home and he didn't want to seem ungrateful. Instead, he nodded at James and gave him a wry smile. He took another sip of his G&T – that wonderful acrid taste, plus lemon and ice cubes; it was delicious.

'I do have an ulterior motive, asking you to stay with me,' James continued. 'In fact probably more than one . . .'

Silence fell as Max waited for him to elaborate. Why was it, he thought, that he tended to end up in the position of waiting for things – people, information? Ever since he had arrived – when, was it only yesterday? – he had felt like a cork tossed about on the sea. But James didn't explain any further. Instead, he just said abruptly, 'But you must be tired after your journey yesterday. I hear the sea got up. I'll show you to your room.'

Max followed him up a flight of wooden stairs at the back of the living room and along a corridor to the side of the building. The corridor's newly burnished floor had been laid immaculately smooth and flat. The floor was hard and echoing, so Max had to place each foot down carefully, the heel first and then the rest of his foot, so as not to make too much noise. James had mastered the art of making no sound at all. The bedrooms all led off the corridor in a row, like private hospital wards.

James led him into the room at the far end of the corridor – a light-filled spacious room overlooking the garden at the back. There was an ornate topiary of abstract, geometric shapes dotted around the lawn. Because of the high sand dunes, the sea was obscured – it was a meditative space, like a room in a healing centre for the terminally ill.

'Dinner will be at nine. Make yourself at home,' James said, before shutting the door behind him.

Max placed his forlorn hold-all on the bed. He took out a block of blank A4 paper, pen and wash bag. The only clothes he had left were the ones he was wearing. He sat down on the bed, then stood up and paced around the room. He went over to the desk and idly opened up the drawers. They were all empty. He tried the door of the wardrobe but it was locked.

He sat down at the desk and picked up his pen – that simple, apparently harmless action filling him with foreboding. This time, his ambition was to write a bestseller, and this required a clinical and calculating mind.

He wrote on the top of a blank page: *Untitled by Max Long*. Then he wrote in capital letters below his name:

IDEAS FOR HORROR BESTSELLER.

'Build-up of suspense, must have beginning, middle and end, and every chapter finish with a cliff-hanger. Must have dramatic first sentence. NO SYMBOLISM. No literariness – that is the work of Lucifer – cf. Milton. Likeable hero that readers can identify with. Bit of a curmudgeon? Perhaps with one or two flaws that provide humour at crucial points? Keep to single horror genre – no one likes a book they can't pigeonhole, do they?'

Max then underlined '*do they?*' three times. Just at that moment there was a huge bang on the window causing Max's heart to miss a beat. It must have been a bird – a sparrow, he thought – and going up to the window he looked down and saw a small brown bird lying immobile on the ground. It was then that a sudden movement in the garden caught his eye. A strange figure was darting about between the elaborately shaped hedges. Max stared into the diminishing light. It looked like a man in dark clothing but what was compelling was the way he was moving. He seemed to be flashing in and out of visibility like a series of stop/start time frames. He then seemed to vanish entirely.

Max returned slowly to his desk, deep in thought.

He was imagining things. He looked down at the ideas he had written down for his bestseller. He didn't know whether to laugh or cry. God, he would have to believe in this project or his book wouldn't be worth the paper it was written on.

In the bathroom, after a quick shower, Max cautiously peered at his face in the mirror. He did *look* like a writer, there was no doubt about that. He had a deep furrow between his brows as well as lines around his mouth and deeper ones around his eyes. He had grey hairs in unkempt brown hair. But the strangest thing of all was the expression that had crept unnoticed, and as if overnight, into his eyes. An expression that belonged to a small, cartoon-like, furry creature of the dark. It was a hopeful but desperate creature, as if it had seen terrible things, and now was trying to recover from having seen them. If he smiled, the creature grinned back at him with Bugs Bunny teeth.

Every time he glanced in the mirror it was a huge shock to Max that he actually looked any older. For writers were life-avoiders. Max hadn't really lived his life, just watched it pass by while making copious notes. He felt only about twenty-five in earth years. But life always took a great big bite out of you in the end. A chunk out of your time on earth when you weren't watching, when you were busy writing your next novel. In writing years, Max was actually about 1027.

He fell asleep on the bed and was woken with a start by a violent knocking on the door.

'Max, it's dinner!' It was James's deep voice.

'Thanks, I'll be down in a minute!'

He splashed some water onto his face and combed a side-parting into his unruly hair. His eyes, when they weren't looking anxious, were definitely his best feature: dark, wide and expressive. He also had reasonable teeth and a smile that could be engaging unless he forgot to concentrate and it collapsed into existential uncertainty.

He ran down the stairs to the living room, where James was sitting at a table that had been recently erected in the centre of the room. To Max's surprise, James was fully dressed in evening dress with white tie. He looked very cavalier, his longish grey hair falling loosely over his forehead. Max sat down opposite him. The silver cutlery glimmered in the candlelight on the white tablecloth. They sat silent for a moment at opposite ends of the table. Max wondered what they were waiting for.

Just then, a young woman walked in, or flowed in as if her body was liquid, carrying a tureen of soup. She had soft brown hair that fell in curls over her shoulders and a logical intense gaze: algebraic eyes. Her skin was cream and her pink cheeks looked as soft as raspberry mousse. She was wearing a severe black shift dress with white collars and white sleeves, which covered her demurely, like a nun's habit. She ladled two spoonfuls of green pea soup into James's bowl, spilling a few drops on the tablecloth as she did so.

She quietly exchanged a secret smile with James before disappearing into the kitchen.

'A lovely girl, Rose,' James said, 'such a boon. She keeps house for me.'

'What does she do exactly?'

'She does many things. All of them well.'

Max looked down, for some reason, at the pea stains on the tablecloth.

'She's a writer, too,' James said.

'Romantic?'

'It's not what you would expect.'

'Erotica?'

James nodded.

'But she seems so sweet,' Max said.

'They always seem sweet at the beginning.'

That night, in a dream, Rose came into Max's bedroom and sat astride him so naturally, her hair falling down over her breasts, her tummy creasing in neat folds, and smelling of lavender and musk.

CHAPTER 4

THE NEXT DAY Max returned to Dr Macdonald's surgery. On this occasion, she was wearing a pressed man's white shirt. Her black linen skirt was stretched tightly over her wide hips. He thought he could detect a certain loucheness about her eyes, or perhaps it was just fatigue.

'It's become infected,' he said triumphantly, sitting down in front of her desk. She lent over the desk and peeled off the dressing roughly and began to poke about.

'Ouch,' he exclaimed.

'You're right,' she said, 'it's become infected. You're going to need some antibiotic cream.'

Disappointed by her dismissive behaviour, after her previous enthusiasm for his writing, he stood up to leave.

'Before you go,' she said, 'is it true you're now staying with James Fairfax?'

He nodded.

'He's very charming,' she said, neutrally.

'He is.'

'Has he got you doing things for him in return, yet?'
Her look was amused.

'No.'

She gave a dry smile that verged on the sinister.

'I should warn you, I wouldn't get too involved with
him.'

'What do you mean?'

'Well, the last time he had a lodger . . .' she trailed
off. Then added, 'And I thought *Lifeblood* was written
in rather an inconsistent style. The ending was tacked
on as if someone else had written it.'

Max had read *Lifeblood*, when it had come out over
a year ago, but his memory of the content was blurred
and confused with the break-up of his marriage. All he
could recall were generalities: the novel's passionate,
impressionistic style.

'But it sold very well,' he said.

'So?'

Max was just about to leave the surgery when Dr
Macdonald called after him, 'Don't forget your ointment!' He picked up the ointment and then, as if
apropos of nothing, she added, 'Would you like to meet
me for a drink, tonight?'

He nodded, trying not to look taken aback.

'Well, there are two pubs on the island. One has
sawdust on the floor; the other is in the hotel.'

'I'll take the one with the carpet.'

'I thought you might. You'll be safer there.' She gave a smile that he thought seemed a little patronising. 'I'll meet you in the foyer at seven . . . Richard is back from the rig. He can put the children to bed.'

'Your husband?'

'Yes, but it's a working arrangement.'

At seven, Max entered the foyer of the hotel. The hotel was an imposing, white-painted, Georgian building on the edge of the sea. Inside, century-old prints of terracotta Burnt Islands hung on the wall. The same man, clearly the laird of the island, was in every print: on his horse, by a boat, in front of the village pub. His face was uncannily like James's. Max was just peering closely to examine the likeness when he heard, 'Why, hello Max!' behind him. He turned round to see Dr Macdonald smiling laconically at him.

She was wearing an off-white trouser suit with a cream ruffled blouse and looked as if she could squeeze between Scylla and Charybdis in one go. She still wore her spectacles on her patrician nose and her thin lips had been coated in coral.

'How are you?' she asked.

'I'm fine.' He smiled.

As he walked with her into the bar, he caught sight

of his reflection in a mirror. He had shaved, his hair was combed and he looked presentable; a bit like a patient on his day out from the asylum. He sat down beside her at a bar table and straightened his back.

'Well, this is nice, Max.' When she wasn't being sardonic, Dr Macdonald had a wonderful smile, like the world was opening up in front of her.

'It is.'

He unconsciously felt his head where he had removed the dressing before coming out. He could feel the scab forming where the seagull had got him with its horny, malevolent beak.

'How is it?' she asked, in a cool manner.

'It's fine, thank you. The ointment has stopped the infection in its tracks.'

'Excellent.'

He looked at her face. 'You're looking pale,' he said to her. It was true she was looking pale, white as a cotton wool swab wrapped in protective plastic.

'I like to keep my face out of direct sunlight. It's not good for the skin. I don't know a single female doctor who doesn't go out without sun cream plastered all over her face.'

It was true, she did look young for her age.

'James doesn't like the sun much either . . .' she added.

He remembered her warning about him that morning.

'You don't seem to like him very much.'

'Oh, it's not a question of *liking*, Max . . . His wife, Natalie, went missing over a couple of years ago. That's bound to leave some kind of trace, don't you think? The Chilean wine looks interesting.'

She laid her hand on the table. He put his hand over hers and she didn't pull hers away.

'What do you want from me, Dr Macdonald?' he asked.

She threw back her head and laughed, her hair falling away to reveal her white neck. There were love bites on it, presumably from the working arrangement she had with her husband who had come off the oil rig.

'Oh, I don't know, Max. Lots of things. Someone to talk to, mainly. Richard is a man of few words. When he's actually here. I long for interesting conversation.'

He felt sorry for her. Under her curt, defensive ugly-duckling manner, she seemed genuinely lonely.

'I'm afraid the only thing us writers want to talk about is money,' he said, laughing. He thought of the horror book he was trying to write, but so much was happening on Burnt Island, it was distracting him from writing it. *Things that had nothing to do with money.*

Dr Macdonald began to gently stroke his palm with

her index finger. Just then her phone rang. She looked down at the flashing screen.

'I'm sorry, Max. I'm on call. I've got to go.'

As he stumbled home alone, fog was settling over the island. He could only just make out the outline of the cypress trees. There was a rustle behind him. The wind in the grass, he thought, or a small animal scurrying through the undergrowth. Then he heard what sounded like someone stumbling over one of the rabbit holes in the dunes. He walked further, brushing through the prickly gorse. Then, that rustling sound again, twenty feet or so behind him. The sound of someone else coming through the gorse. Max felt his breath grow shallower and his heart beat faster. *Someone in the fog was following him.*

A blackbird issuing a shrill warning call darted out of a bush in front of him. After the echo of the bird's call had died away, silence fell, no sound of footsteps. Had the footsteps just been the echo of his own steps? He started walking again, making his strides deliberately slower and longer, but the steps that started up behind him were short and quick.

The clammy, soft fog was whirling around the island in enticing shapes. Now, even the tops of the trees had disappeared under the grey mist. He wanted to turn around, but was too afraid to encounter whatever it was behind him. He reached the garden. He thought he could make out the outline of a figure – it looked like a man – beneath the cypress trees ahead of him. 'Who's that?' he shouted out. 'Is that you, James?'

But there was no reply.

'Who *are* you?' he shouted out again. '*Say* something.'

But the figure just turned and started to walk towards the shore, into the grey sea of fog.

That evening, as the two male writers ate, Max could see an intensely tender look come into James's eyes, while Rose bent over him to serve supper. His gaze was also proprietorial. Rose's role in the home seemed to be more surrogate wife than housekeeper. Max wondered if she had become a kind of platonic replacement for James's missing wife, Natalie. However, Rose quietly left the table before they started eating.

As Max was tucking into the roast pheasant with chestnut stuffing, James said, 'Max, I do worry Burnt Island may be distracting you from your own writing.'

'Don't worry,' Max said. 'I'm sure the ideas will come soon.'

'Nothing worse than nothing to do,' said James. 'Can drive a man over the brink.'

'Yes, writers are always just on the edge of having nothing to do.'

'Ah,' said James, 'indeed. That narrow line between a literary masterpiece and a blank piece of paper. We all need that piece of grit in the mussel to produce the final pearl.'

James gave an enigmatic smile that made Max feel for an insane moment *he* was James's piece of grit.

Perhaps James was going to base one of the characters in his new book on him. James, like all writers, would be more magpie than human – especially if he was starting on a new book and looking for sparkling new people to line his nest. He would focus on the flawed – virtuous people were not so interesting; anyone can be good, but people can be bad in so many ways.

Max was certainly flawed but he was hardly sparkling. He was like a hamster on his wheel, a nocturnal, lonely creature smelling of straw and old fur, rotating forlornly in his cage. It occurred to him, if the worst came to worst and his next book was a failure, he would force himself to stop writing altogether, take the wheel out of the cage – in fact why stop there? – open the door to the cage with his ink-stained paw and escape into the shimmering moonlight.

He felt faint as if his skin was peeling off and he was ceasing to be who he was.

'Are you all right?'

James was looking at him anxiously. Max could feel sweat pouring from his face. He was still chewing a piece of pheasant he had put in his mouth five minutes ago. He swallowed it too quickly and immediately started choking. He took a gulp of water, spluttering.

'I'm fine.'

'You seemed lost in your thoughts. And then you went white as a sheet.'

'No, really, I'm fine – what are *you* working on at the moment, James?'

'I don't really like to discuss my work in public, Max. People might steal my ideas. I have to be careful, Max. Very careful, generally, whom I talk to, whom I let into my home.'

The Meerkat had told Max that James had been a banker before writing *Lifeblood,* and Max wondered if his experience in the city had created this cautiousness. However, James then proceeded to regale him with hilarious personal anecdotes of famous literary writers he had met at literature festivals and how he had shared late night drinks with them at the plush hotels they had stayed in. 'An intense affinity and rapport builds up quickly,' he explained and smiled at Max gently. Then he told Max the story of the male Man Booker prize winner who had seduced the chicklit author and then boasted he had dropped her like a stone after reading one of her books because it had had too many clichés in it.

Max listened intently, as if by some vicarious magic he had become part of this shining, literary universe. How he longed to be part of this world. He didn't want to keep struggling on alone, ungarlanded. He wanted James's life; more he wanted to *be* James.

Max imagined the flowers James's publisher would have sent him on publication day. Not ordinary flowers – carnations or daffodils squeezed into a cellophane cone – but flowers as a work of art, orchids wrought into strange ornate shapes. Flowers that were tax deductible.

Max pictured the launch party for *Lifeblood*. All the infamous literary critics of the day would have come to pay James homage. Gorgeous women like the Meerkat's last few wives would have gravitated towards him, for there is no more magnetic appeal to a beautiful, clever woman than a writer with money.

He, however, was growing older and the happiness he had thought he could find in his writing was ebbing away as if through a small wound in his thigh. But Max struggled gamely on, as if it was the only thing he could do. And it was. Coming to Burnt Island was his last-chance saloon.

That evening, Max found himself sitting on his bed in his room, staring at the wardrobe, whose locked doors seemed to be staring back at him. He stood up, walked over to the wardrobe, gripped the handle and pulled at the doors again. This time he kept pulling until the lock snapped with a spasmodic crack. The door swung open.

Inside the wardrobe was hanging a soft Italian suit covered in a light tracing of dust. Max searched the jacket pockets and pulled out a handwritten medical prescription, a fountain pen and a leather-bound note-book. He examined the prescription. It was written out by a Dr Macdonald for a Daniel Levy – presumably the previous lodger. The prescription was for a drug Max didn't recognise. He opened up the notebook. It was blank except for a couple of lines scrawled on the first page:

The whole thing is impossible. But the way she gazes at me. Her hair looks on fire in the sun.

Before falling asleep, Max imagined monsters coming out from the sea at night. Monsters with blood eyes and black scales and flickering tails. Definite shapes, angry and volatile, that were crawling over the island. He woke up and heard a creature moving about in his room. He sat up in his bed. 'Who's there?' There was a hissing sound and then a terrible stench. 'Who is there?' he asked again, his limbs cold, as if turned to stone. His eyes felt heavy, as if he were going to fall asleep again through fear, or just lose consciousness. 'Get out,' Max whispered. *'Get out of my room.'* He then lay awake, in that time during the night when it is just you and reality, and reality is winning.

CHAPTER 5

AT BREAKFAST THE next morning, Rose shouted through from the kitchen, 'We should go on a picnic!' and then she came out of the kitchen, carrying an old-fashioned, wicker picnic-basket. There was an ineffable quality about Rose that touched Max, an unusual lack of self-consciousness. She was wearing a navy blue, cotton dress and the look on her face suggested she was genuinely excited to see him. She looked briefly over the ill-fitting Italian suit he was wearing.

Max felt good; a few days on the island and he felt healthier than he had done in years. There was a flush to his cheeks and he felt leaner.

'Here, let me take this.'

He took the basket. It was surprisingly heavy and wrenched his elbow.

'What have you got in here?'

'The picnic,' she replied. There *was indeed* a wondrous simplicity to her.

They set off for the dunes, the sun shining. Rose seemed to know exactly where she was going. They followed a narrow path through the dunes, which widened out into a sheltered spot on the beach, surrounded by banks on three sides. It was reassuringly private but had a wonderful, open view of the azure sea. Max lay down in the sand, the sun blazing down onto his face, and started to daydream.

He had one of those daydreams that seem to happen just below the glittery, watery surface of waking life. He had just spotted Rose walking away from him over a bridge. They were on Burnt Island but it was part of the island he had never seen before with grassy meadows brimming with wildflowers and lined by trees. He started to run, wanting to catch her attention, delighted he had seen her by accident, here. He shouted out her name. But when she turned around he was shocked to see not Rose, but James's face smiling engagingly back at him. Roused from his daydream, Max looked up to see Rose, clear-skinned and healthy, lying on a rug beside him, reading *The Shining*.

'Do you want a ham sandwich?' she asked and handed him one.

He took a bite; the bread was fresh and crusty and slightly sugary, the ham pink with a single thread of sweet fat, and the mustard was grainy hot. It was a sensual experience of the highest order eating that ham sandwich: the conflicting textures of the soft bread, with the resistant ham in the creamy mustard.

He had never tasted a sandwich like it. As he ate, the sea air blew against his face, mingling with the flavour of the sandwich.

He found Rose staring at him, hard.

'You do know, James hardly likes anyone. But he likes you. He definitely likes you. You're one of these people who don't realise how fundamentally well-meaning they are. You'd never hurt anyone.'

'I've hurt people unintentionally,' Max said, quietly. 'Who hasn't?'

'Well, I'm flattered that James likes me,' Max said.

'He grew extremely fond of Daniel, too.'

'The previous lodger?'

'Yes.'

He caught a note of uncertainty in her voice.

'What did he need a prescription for?' Max asked. 'I found one in a suit he left behind.'

'While he was staying here, he became paranoid – convinced he was being followed, stuff like that.'

Rose leapt to her feet. 'Luckily, I don't believe in monsters. I'm going for a swim.' And she disappeared behind the dunes.

When she didn't reappear, Max decided to follow her into the dunes.

≈

Reaching the top of one of the highest dunes that over-looked the sea to the west, Max came upon five large, upright stones standing in a circle. Engraved on the stones, in indecipherable script, was faded lettering. What Max found intriguing about ancient monuments were their imperfections, but as he approached the circle, he noticed an abnormal symmetry. He remembered how difficult it had been to draw circles in school art lessons. How they had curved or turned into ovals or misshapen bumps. Only Giotto could draw a perfect circle.

Max turned to look at the dark blue sea and when he looked around again one of the stones had moved out of the circle, to make a disjointed line. The circle had been perfect and now it was not, as the sea ebbed and flowed on the beach. He could not believe the evidence of his own eyes. It was as if a trauma of perception had torn at the membrane of his life until reality was peeping through, bright and vivid and hard. That was the trouble with reality, he thought, *it was just too real* for him.

He tentatively approached the shifting stone. It was entrenched in the grass and earth and sand, as the other stones were. But it was no longer part of the circle. No soil had been disturbed, there were no lines in the grass, *no wheels.* Had he been mistaken? Had his initial perception of a perfect circle of standing stones been wrong? He walked back in the direction of the picnic site, took a deep breath and looked back at the stones. The stones now stood, lonely sentinels in the distance, in a perfect circle.

He returned to their picnic site on the beach to find Rose standing waiting for him, wearing a scarlet one-piece swimming costume. There were no details on her costume, no frills or metal hoops. She didn't need any adornment. She adorned herself. The surface of her was very smooth. He remembered teaching Luke as a toddler to swim in the sea, remembered his son's unadulterated joy at being in the open water. Max's had felt his son's happiness as his own so sharply, it had turned his breath to glass.

Rose ran down into the sea and he watched her swim for a while, her white body bobbing up and down like a porpoise between the waves. She then waded out of the water again, dripping wet, and walked up the beach as if enjoying every step her foot took in the hot sand, every caress of the cool breeze that wafted onto her skin, every sensuous drop of salt water falling from her limbs. She walked right up to where he was lying on the sand and stood above him, the expanse of her pale skin like a cloud, her costume like the blinding sun. Her body looked as if it had been carved out of the situation – the ancient stones, the blue sky and the distant roar of the Atlantic. She lay down beside him on her side, her body arched.

'I've come here to *write*,' Max found himself saying.

'Of course you have,' she said.

Just then they heard footsteps. Rose leapt up and quickly pulled her dress on over her costume, as a man, his fair hair glinting in the sun, approached. It was Ryan.

'I was looking for you, Rose. What are you doing here?'

He was staring at Max suspiciously.

'Just having a picnic,' Rose replied.

Ryan quickly flashed a smile and took her hand roughly.

Max, groping around in his head for some words to delay Rose going, said, 'Any time you want me to take a look at your writing . . .'

'Oh, yeah, thanks, Max.'

She gave him an innocent smile.

Max watched, as the two young lovers disappeared out of sight. He felt, mingled with his sadness at Rose going, a fleeting, amorphous fear.

Slowly, he walked back towards the house. He could hear the Atlantic beating on the shore. A blustery wind had started up. He wondered how Natalie had gone missing. Surely, on an island, it would be difficult for someone to disappear without anyone noticing. Someone must have seen *something* suspicious. He could see the small pier his ferry had moored at. Natalie could have set off from there by boat, and no one would have seen her go.

Having entered the huge living room, he looked around at the tasteful black and white photographs hanging on the walls, to see if he could find a picture of Natalie. But there were just photographs of James at various triumphant moments over the course of his life – graduating from Cambridge, becoming Chairman of the bank, and winning various literary awards. James hadn't changed much over the years – extremely handsome men or beautiful women weren't ravaged by age as much as normal people, Max had begun to observe.

There were no photographs of Natalie.

CHAPTER 6

MAX BELIEVED HE would sell his soul to the devil for his next novel to become a bestseller, if only the devil existed, if only Max could just bump into him and get him to make an offer. This ambition for his work was eating away at him. He began wondering about the exact nature of a Faustian pact. What would he do to make it, what would it take?

At dinner, waiting for James to come down, Max wondered what the devil would look like – plausible, without doubt, plausible, like an artist, he would have to convince you of his lies. He would also have a sense of the absurdity of his own existence. Why was he thinking these nonsensical thoughts, Max wondered? He didn't believe in the devil. He hardly believed in evil – just the banality of man. But evil *per se* in the shape of an archetype? It was this island making him think these thoughts – the roaring of the sea was playing with his mind, like a fiend crying out for his soul.

But sometimes he did wonder if the devil existed. Writing the first drafts of his previous books, Max would sometimes feel in the grip of a demonic possession. It would dictate to him convoluted dreams that he could only translate afterwards. But his next novel, written on Burnt Island, would have nothing to do with satanic creativity. It would be written by the rational god of market forces.

Max rubbed his eyes vigorously. When he lowered his hands, there was James, sitting at the end of the dining table, smiling in his usual, avuncular manner.

'You know, Max, this is your chance to write the book you've always wanted to write, on Burnt Island. Without compromise. Have you any idea how impressive you are? The way you keep churning out the types of novel you do? Against all the odds? In spite of so little reward? What integrity that shows, what belief in your art?'

Max hadn't told James about his secret plan to write a bestseller because he knew any respect James had for him would have evaporated like a snowflake on the back of his hand.

'You mean write a book like my other ones?' Max asked.

'You can go even further.'

'Make them even more unreadable?'

'Unreadable only to the prejudiced. The lazy. The loveless.'

Max was touched – few people had shown such

faith in him, certainly not his ex-wife, his ex-publisher, his only-just-not-ex-agent. Only Luke had shown unswerving faith in him, had told him, 'Soon, Dad, it will happen for you. It's fate!' His father hadn't the heart to tell him fate had nothing to do with commitment and was only tenuously connected to desire.

Of course, as Dot and his previous publishers constantly whispered in his ear, '*No one is making you do this.*' But they didn't understand. Of course someone was making him do this. *He was making him do this*.

Listening to James's urgings, Max grew even more confused about his plans to compromise. Here was one of the country's most successful writers, telling him to do what he had always done, but more so. He felt torn. He had been set on his new path and now wondered whether it was the right path. He rallied – he must remain focused. His bestseller must appeal to millions, be full of sex and terror and *character development*.

The two men tucked into their rhubarb crumble, deliciously sweet and tart at the same time.

'So, do you have any ideas for your next book?' James was asking.

Max thought fast. 'I'm planning to use the symbolism of the words "Burnt Island" to explore our fear of mortality.'

James looked impressed.

'I love your use of symbolism,' James said.

'Readers don't.'

'Who cares about the readers? James Joyce wrote for only one reader. *The ideal reader.*'

It was all very well for *James Fairfax* to be saying this, thought Max, with his one million bloody readers.

'The trouble with one ideal reader,' Max said, 'is it means only £9.99 for two years of work . . . But it's not just the symbolism of the words I want to use. There's something intriguing about the actual island.'

'Intriguing?' James looked surprised. 'In what way?'

'I don't know. Things don't seem quite right.'

'You mean, out of place?'

'Things seem slightly slanted to the left.'

'And you want to straighten us up?'

'I'm hardly the person to do that.'

'You're off centre.'

'Exactly.'

James laughed, the candlelight flickering between them. Max felt they were experiencing a strange correspondence of minds.

'It was odd. I was in the dunes the other day. Amongst the standing stones,' Max said.

James looked amused. 'Ah yes, the standing stones.'

Max hesitated, wondering whether to continue.

Encouraged by the older man's expectant look, he went on.

'It was bizarre. Mad, even. One of the stones seemed to move.'

James looked at him, suddenly alert. Had he stumbled on a supernatural event, or was James just thinking he'd gone insane?

James said quietly, 'Trick of the light, old boy, I'm sure.'

'No one's ever mentioned to you anything like that?'

'You mean a standing stone going for a walk? No, I can't say they have.'

'There's no story about the stones, then?'

James paused. 'You mean some ancient lore? Now I come to think of it, I think there is. A villager mentioned something about it to me once. Something about a broken circle symbolising betrayal: the betrayal of a loved one.' James laughed. 'Had you had one too many drinks perhaps?'

'It's what I saw.'

'That's what I like about you, Max – the way you see. You're an original. It's just your imagination, Max – best put it into one of your books.

'Life is built on illusion, isn't it? An illusion of our immortality. How on earth can we go around every day knowing we're going to die? We're prey to illusion –

it's essential to our sanity. We must, of necessity, have our fantasies. We all have various dreams to different degrees. As a writer you'll always suffer from a greater degree of illusion than most people.'

James, the man of letters, looked at him, his eyes twinkling in the candlelight, the white damask table-cloth lightly stained pink where some drops of his red wine had fallen.

'I'm going to bed now,' James said. 'You're welcome to stay up for a while and muse.'

Max remained sitting at the table, listening to the sea crashing against the rocks outside the luxurious glass-house he now inhabited. The good food in his stomach, the fire burning in the grate and a pleasant feeling of inebriation were all contributing to a sense of content-ment he had not felt in a long time.

Just then there was an animal shriek. Max was sure it came from somewhere in the house. It had been a piercing cry – hardly human. It sounded like the screech of a fox. He began to feel uneasy. At night, the large plate-glass windows overlooking the sea left the expansive living room feeling exposed.

In bed, that night, he dreamt a succubus came to him. Voluptuous with dark hair, she rode astride him viciously until he came, panting and sweating. Her breasts were round and high, like the distant moon shining through his window in the sky. He woke drenched in perspiration, his and hers, as heat poured through every inch of his body, scalding the surface of his skin.

CHAPTER 7

MAX CLIMBED DOWN the steps the following day to Rose's self-contained apartment in the basement of the house. Her small living room was overshadowed by the high dunes that surrounded the back of the house but in spite of the darkness the room was intricately feminine. Cream lacy curtains framed the dainty, fairy-tale windows. Delicate crystal pendants hung from the ceiling and giant, paper butterflies sunbathed on the pastel-coloured walls. The furniture was draped in suggestive folds of cerise fabrics such as chiffon and silk, and pretty scarlet lampshades cast an intimate glow over the room. Max had never seen a room so full of softness. He found the atmosphere the opposite of comforting – it was discombobulating, as if he had slipped into someone else's dream.

I have spread my dreams under your feet;
Tread softly because you tread on my dreams.

'Can I get you a drink?' Rose asked.
   'A glass of white wine?'

She disappeared into the kitchen. He quickly glanced down at her desk. Lying on the desktop was a handwritten draft of an unfinished manuscript. Before Max could pick the draft up, Rose had come back into the room. She put a bottle of wine on the table.

'So you're taking after James?' he asked, still standing by her desk.

She looked puzzled. 'Sorry?'

'I mean you write, too.'

She looked angry. 'Were you reading my work?'

'I thought you wanted me to.'

'I've changed my mind.'

She went up to him and slowly put her arms around his neck. Underneath her sensuality, her vulnerability was like a shimmering shadow, grey and glittering – a miasma that surrounded her physical body. Max was distinctly attuned to fragility.

He thought of Luke and how his writing had always taken precedence over his son. How it had stolen time away from him. When Luke had needed his father like a sunflower needs the rain, Max had remained locked away in his study. Luke had asked for attention in both direct and indirect ways and in the end had withdrawn from his father entirely. Max took a step back from Rose, gently pulling her arms down from his neck.

'Rose, I'm sorry. It just doesn't feel right.' He hesitated. 'And there's Ryan.'

'What you really mean, Max, is "And there's Dad".'

'I don't understand.'

She looked surprised 'Oh, I thought you'd realised. James is my father.'

'Oh.'

'I help him out.'

Max frowned.

'I know it's odd we didn't tell you,' Rose continued, 'but we didn't mean to keep it secret. We're just very private, that's all. Especially since Mum went missing. You'd have found out soon enough, anyway.'

'So he won't mind?'

'Anything happening between us? I wouldn't think so. I mean, he won't hold it against you. It won't stop him helping you or anything, if that's what you're worried about.'

'I'm not so sure,' Max said.

Rose acted like her father's wife, cooked and prepared the meals, supervised the running of the house. He had even seen her book his flights to London.

As if reading his thoughts again, she said, 'I know we seem very close for a father and daughter but Dad needs me. After Mum disappeared, Dad changed.'

'And you never talk about her with him?'

'He doesn't like to talk about her. When I ask, he just says something gnomic like, "She'd been missing a long time before she actually disappeared." When I try to delve further he just mutters unintelligibly. Or else tears well up in his eyes. So I stop.'

A huge sadness was apparent in her eyes. And Max felt for her. He thought of Luke and how lucky it was his son had a mother like Dot and how different he would have been without her.

'What was Natalie like?' he asked.

'She was searching for something she could never find.'

'She sounds like the sort of person who *would* go missing.'

'Only in retrospect,' Rose said. 'You never think it's going to happen until it does.'

'So you do think she's dead?'

Rose looked at him. 'It's the only explanation. Otherwise I know she would have got in contact with us. I just know. She never would have stayed away from us for so long and not sent a card or phoned just to let us know she was OK, to check we were OK. It's just not possible. We tried everything. The police searched the whole island. Contacted the mainland. There were search parties for her involving all the islanders. Nothing.'

She looked at the bottle of wine still standing on the table. 'I've forgotten the glasses.' As she returned to the kitchen, Max glanced down at the manuscript lying on her desk again. He quickly slid out a page of Rose's slanted writing. It was only just legible:

The only incongruous object in the room was a large, empty bookcase standing against one of the walls. Turning to go back up the steps, he switched off the light. But a chink of light still shone into the room. The light was coming from underneath the bookcase. Max walked over to the bookcase and, with the lightest of touches, it silently swung open.

The stone walls of the hidden room behind the bookcase were painted black and shackles were attached to the floors and walls. It was intensely claustrophobic as if instead of walking into a room Max had walked into another's innermost private thoughts, thoughts of perverted desire. But these thoughts were real, they had been acted out, one by one, most deliberately. These thoughts had chains on them, had worn shackles and had cried out and bled with pleasure and pain.

Max was full of wonderment at people who actually acted out their desires. He had spent his whole life keeping his desires once removed either through fear or thwarted ambition. He put his desires into books or put his obsessional thoughts into dreams of his literary success.

A monstrous metal bed dominated the room with satanic imagery painted in lurid colours on the large embossed metal headboard. Pictures of contorted satyric figures sucked the blood from voluptuous, naked women but it was the real, naked woman on the bed that drew Max's attention.

Max couldn't see the young woman's face but could make out the hair – chestnut curls – and the gentle curve of her hips. A naked man was standing beside her with his back to the door, his grey hair falling loosely about his shoulders. Max quietly closed the bookcase behind him.

He quickly slipped the page back, disconcerted by the dark content and also by the calling of one of her characters Max. Was it just a coincidence? It made him feel uncertain of her. When she returned from the kitchen, holding two glasses, he was already standing by the door, about to leave.

∾

Later that evening, when Max was alone in the living room, the phone rang. He recognised the soft, controlled voice of his fourteen-year-old son. Intense feelings of protectiveness welled up inside him.

'Hi, Dad.'

'Hi, Luke.'

'How are you doing, Dad? How's Burnt Island? Sounds fun.'

Max was always amazed at how quickly the roles between father and son were inverted. It had taken all of ten words.

'Does it?'

'Well, it's a weird name to begin with.'

'You mean it has connotations of fire?'

'Yeah. Right up your street.'

'What do you mean exactly?'

'I don't mean you're a pyrotechnic. I mean you like to destroy things.'

'OK, Luke, that's enough.'

That was the only time when he felt like a real father, now. When he was stopping his son from insulting him.

'Can I come out and visit you?'

'Where?'

'Burnt Island.'

'Not sure if that's a good idea, Luke. It's time for me

to write, you see. A chance for me to concentrate on my new novel. Get some solid work done. At least a first draft. You'd only disturb my concentration, you know that. It would be better if you didn't.'

He didn't want to tell Luke the real reason he didn't want him to come, that there was a strangeness about the place that made him feel it would be dangerous for Luke to visit.

'OK,' Luke said in a small voice of meek acceptance that caused Max to be consumed with guilt. Luke had learnt to acknowledge that his father's career took precedence. Had honed over the years his skill in swallowing his disappointment whole, like a snake digesting a baby bison with horns.

A few minutes after he had put down the phone to Luke, it rang again. It was Dot.

'I've just spoken to Luke. He's upset.'

'Oh. Something you said?'

'No. Something *you* said.'

That familiar note of contempt that, in the last months of their marriage, had been the only mode in which she had communicated with him.

'What have I done?'

'Try and guess.'

'But I explained it all to him. It's supposed to be a retreat. *For writing*.' He didn't want to worry Dot with his suspicions about the island, either. His fears were so unformed. Nor did he want to confirm to her what she had always thought about him. How he could verge on the delusional.

'For writing another book that won't sell. Can't you for once put your son first?'

'Dot,' he said through gritted teeth, 'I promise if this books fails I'll get a sensible job. Advertising. Civil service. Garage mechanic.' Actually, that *was* quite sensible. 'Luke understands he can't come,' Max continued. 'He's very grown up. He's a credit to you.'

'Don't patronise me. I hate it when you patronise me. It's your way of manipulating me.'

'I was just paying you a compliment.'

'Well, don't.'

'Look, Dot. I need peace and quiet on the island. Solitude. It's going to be no fun for Luke. It's going to be boring. Just me being boring and looking for inspiration. You know what *that's* like.'

Dot fell silent, again. He could hear her remembering what that was like.

'I'll try and explain it to him,' she said finally.

'Thanks, Dot. You're a star.'

'*Don't* patronise me.'

'OK. Say sorry to Luke for me.'

'God, you're annoying!'

'I don't mean to be.'

'That's the *really* annoying bit. You have no idea how annoying you are.'

'Bye.'

'Bye, Max. Good luck with the writing.'

Never had he heard so much irony in a voice. It was the irony of accumulated resentment pressed into those few words like a Volvo concertinaed by an automated crusher in a car dump. This was not the real Dot, he thought, after they had hung up. This was her doppelgänger.

After his conversations with Luke and Dot, he needed some fresh air and went out for a walk in the garden. He was ambling along by one of the hedges when his eye was caught by an ashen object on the ground. Over a foot long, white and smooth, it looked like a bone, a human bone. He stared at it. It couldn't be. Venison perhaps from a barbecue. His writer's mind was imagining things again. He picked it up gingerly. The bone definitely looked like a human femur. He dropped it again. There was an odd smell emanating from it, sweet and pungent. I'm getting carried away, he thought.

He often thought his imagination was a curse rather than a blessing, the way it obscured reality. He blundered around imaginary obstacles, only to trip over the real obstacles lying under the sand the whole time, spiky and hard, ready to pierce his heart, all of a sudden.

CHAPTER 8

ROSE BROUGHT RYAN home to meet James. Her
father was elaborately polite, which impressed Max
because Ryan had hardly cleaned up from the garage
and his clothes were oil stained. There was also grime
under his fingernails. But if this offended James's
natural sense of good manners, he didn't show it.

'So, this is a nice place, James,' said Ryan with his
mouth open to reveal pieces of rabbit and mushy peas
churning around inside.

'Thank you, Ryan. I designed it myself.'

Max was about to blurt out the name of the real
architect, but stopped himself in time. He was surprised at the lie, didn't think James was the sort of
person to stoop to lying to impress his daughter's
boyfriend.

He looked at Rose, who was giving her father a dis-
approving look, and – like Max – was not saying anything to contradict him. She and Max were now lying
too, he thought, lying by omission. That was often what
happened if you hung around liars; they made you lie
too.

'So how is your garage getting on, Ryan?' James asked.

'Fine, thanks, James.'

Ryan continued eating. Ryan was a man of few words. Max was aware of a strange atmosphere in the room but couldn't work out where the tension was coming from. James seemed polite, Rose vague and Ryan nonchalant to the point of insolence. There was now so much tension in the room, Max was starting to feel ill. Perhaps it was coming from him. He tended to generate emotion like electricity. Every time he thought he couldn't summon another emotion up – had his emotions not been *exhausted*? – another one sprang up.

'This is delicious, Rose,' Ryan said.

James said proudly, 'Rose is a very good cook.'

Max saw Rose look at James in a way she had never looked at him or Ryan – with an expression of open adoration. She was looking particularly vibrant tonight: she was like a budding plant speeded up a thousand times. James saw Max looking at her. *Had James seen his sudden longing?*

'Rose,' James suggested suddenly, 'why don't you tell Max the story of William Hazlitt? The man who made Shakespeare famous.'

Rose laughed. 'OK, Dad. I know the story you mean.

It's a cautionary tale. Poor William Hazlitt. He fell passionately in love with his landlady's daughter. But only after her mother had asked her to flirt with all the lodgers in order to keep them in the house. When Hazlitt found out he was being used, he had a nervous breakdown. He grew so thin and lost so much hair, his friends only recognised him when he smiled.'

'And why that story in particular, James?' Max asked.

'Oh, I don't know. It's kind of sad and funny at the same time,' James said, 'don't you think?'

That evening, after Ryan had left, Max looked out of his bedroom window at the cypress trees, the garden and its topiary hedges, and they all seemed to be saying to him it was now too late for him. Max was consumed by a sense of longing that seemed to connect his growing desire for Rose with his jealousy of James's wealth and literary success.

Over the next few days, his longing for Rose intensified. But he was wary – he didn't want to sabotage his relationship with her father. And there was also Ryan, who operated in the generic not the specific, which just served to give him more masculine power. But in the end, these obstacles only made Rose more desirable. He began carrying around his longing like a quartz crystal inside him: shiny, white, sharp and heavy. Actually, it was more like his heart had turned to crystal.

James's secrecy about his writing had made Max curious; if only he could read an early draft of James's next novel it might inspire him in the writing of his own. It would not be a matter of plagiarism. Reading Fairfax's work would be more like the casting of a voodoo spell imbuing Max with the power to write and enchant the reader as *Lifeblood* had.

James had left the island to visit the Meerkat in London. Max waited until he heard Rose leave the house, then quietly opened his bedroom door. Overcome by nervous anticipation at the idea of reading James's unedited words, Max crept down to James's study, at the far end of the corridor. There would be pages of deletions, added or subtracted adjectives, the unadulterated sum of his thoughts. Max would be able to physically, touch – like a fetish – James's first draft.

But to Max's disappointment, the top of James's desk was clear. There was no sign of a novel in progress at all. Max pulled down one of the books from the single shelf over the desk and opened it. The novel – a classic – had been closely marked and underlined with 'use this' occasionally scribbled in the margins, or certain descriptions of characters heavily marked. He took down another book. Similar intensive markings had been made, as if a spider with inky feet had run over the pages. So this was how James was constructing his next novel – using other books as a blueprint for his own. Max was bemused: *Lifeblood* had been described as 'vivid and startlingly original' by the *New York Review of Books*.

And then a bizarre thought struck Max. Was it possible that James was not the author of *Lifeblood*? James tended to talk about his writing in a very abstract way. But if James was not the writer, who was? And what did that make James?

There was a sudden sharp poke in his back. Max looked around. A little girl of about nine stood full square in front of him, her chin up in the air. Her fragile, bony face had colourless, protruding eyes, which were emphasised by the pulling-back of her thin mousey hair in an Alice band. It was the same girl who had scared the seagulls away.

'I wandered in here by mistake. I thought it was my bedroom,' Max said, suddenly aware, by the way the girl was staring at him, that he should not have been in James's study. 'All the doors look the same,' he added.

She was still gazing at him, her young forehead deeply furrowed. *Why didn't she say anything?* She took his hand and slowly walked him out of the room to his own bedroom. Outside his door, she turned around and walked back down the corridor without uttering a word.

James was still away in London when Rose came down to dinner wearing a dark-purple dress covered in silver stars, making her look like the night sky. Her hair was loosely tied back and her lips painted pink. In the candlelight she looked as if she were flickering with a secret emotion. The red undertones of her chestnut hair were catching the light in flashes of flame.

She sat down in James's seat. When Max looked at women, he felt a disjunction between their beauty and their minds, how they seemed and what they were. Their beauty he could objectively admire but their minds and emotions were like quicksand to him. Sometimes he found it difficult to desire and understand women at the same time. In fact, he had no particular interest in doing so. But there was an atmosphere about the island that was making him feel more impulsive, younger – *as he would like to be again*. He felt in his twenties again, but with the added wisdom and experience to make him fully appreciate this sensation of youth.

And the way Rose was looking at him. Her pupils were dilated and her face strangely still, as if immobilised by desire. Or was he just imagining this? She would smell of flowers, he thought. All over. Inside and out. When he desired her, she no longer seemed so complicated. '*I'm yours*,' suddenly flashed into his mind as she was looking at him. It sounded like her voice but he couldn't be sure; it could have been his.

'I'm sorry, I didn't catch that,' he said, trying to find out.

'I didn't say anything,' she replied.

He no longer cared that she was James's daughter. She was grown up, after all. He too was – in theory – grown up. Why should James mind? Why should he even find out? They could decide (initially) to keep it secret. As for the moment, James was far away and Ryan was Ryan. Max walked over and stood behind Rose as she remained seated. She started to speak softly, her back still to him.

'Sometimes I think I can hear a Siren song coming from the sea. An irresistible sound, the song of my imagination. When the Sirens sing out they confuse what is real and what is not. I think that's what happened to her.'

'You mean to Natalie?' he asked

'She could have heard them sing and they lured her

into the sea. At night sometimes the sea shimmers with their song.'

'Shimmers?'

'Yes. Like moonlight. When there is no moon. And they hum.'

'Hum?'

'A vibration. Like music . . .' She laughed. 'You're sounding worried. Don't worry. I know the Sirens are just in my imagination. But I should warn you, Burnt Island is a place where your imagination can come alive.'

'What, at any time?'

'It tends to be when you're daydreaming.'

'That's me, most of the time.'

'The illusions start off OK. Can be like sexual fantasies. But they can turn. Become difficult.'

'It's enough to drive you mad,' Max said, thinking privately that that was what had already happened to Rose. But her strange ideas just intensified her erotic aura. Her body didn't seem so much of a suggestion as a downright demand.

She stood up and turned around to face him. Her bare legs and arms were the colour of pale sand. He kissed her gently at first and then more intently. Her arms around his neck were as light as a feathered wing. He stroked the back of her neck below where the whorls began, her skin soft and taut, like the skin of a drum. He could feel her give in to the sensation, just a slight shift downwards. He felt down her back to its hollow. She shifted her hips towards him. Her face was flushed.

'Let's go upstairs,' she whispered.

In his room, she lay down on his bed, her purple chiffon dress riding up in folds above her thighs.

'Rose, Rose, Rose,' he whispered.

'Max, Max, Max,' she said, taunting him.

He pulled her dress down over one of her shoulders and began kissing her bare skin as she began to unbelt his trousers. There was a resilient pounding in his head. *No, it was not in his head.* There was a pounding *on the door*. Someone was knocking on the door.

He hastily got up, panic-stricken – was it James? Rose whispered urgently, 'Ignore it, Max, they'll go away,' but the knocking persisted and Max, frustrated and angry, began buckling up his belt. Rose sighed petulantly and turned away from him onto her side. She very deliberately picked up a book from his bedside table and started to read. Now her back was to him, Max could see fresh, lurid, red welts on the back of her bare shoulder.

Max opened the door. There standing confrontationally in the shadows wearing polka-dotted blue and white pyjamas was the young girl. He looked at her. She held up a small book-sized black board on which was written, in chalk, *I heard sounds from Rose's bedroom. Like she was being attacked*.

Max suddenly realised she was mute. Her accusatory stare remained unwavering.

'She was,' Max said, ominously. 'By me.'

She looked at him, puzzled at the lack of guilt he was showing, and wrote, *Can I come in?*

'What, to check if she's still alive?' he asked.

She looked more outraged than upset. Max wearily opened the door further. Rose looked up from reading her book.

'Hi, Esther.' Rose gave a fixed smile. 'What are you doing here?'

'I've told Esther already – I've been attacking you,' Max announced.

'He's being silly,' Rose said. 'Of course he didn't attack me. We were just having an interesting conversation. Now go back to bed.'

Esther shook her head.

'You're scared?' Rose asked.

She nodded.

'There's no need to be scared,' Rose said, trying to conceal a look of concern. Rose glanced at Max to see if he'd noticed and he pretended he hadn't.

'Don't be silly, now. Go to bed. It's late,' Rose told her, firmly.

Esther reluctantly shut the door behind her and they heard her little footsteps fading away down the corridor. Rose got up from the bed, pulled her dress back up over her shoulder and ran her hands through her hair.

'Who is Esther?' Max asked. 'Your sister?' he added, sarcastically.

'Actually, she is. For the past year, during school term, she has been staying with a friend's family on the island.'

Max felt this was more and more like a dream, where people appear out of nowhere and in retrospect are given significance by the dreamer. Rose had suddenly become James's daughter and now this odd little girl had become Rose's sister. Somehow these revelations were not reassuring.

'Why doesn't she stay with you all the time?'

'Dad felt she needed a mother figure after Mum went missing. And he doesn't like to be disturbed while he's writing. Esther can be a bit inquisitive. But during the holidays she comes back to live with us. Esther is an absolute innocent, she knows nothing about the real world. She's young. She's protected here. We all protect her.'

It all sounded unlikely. Protected from what, Max wondered? What was there to protect her from on Burnt Island?

'Esther is special,' Rose continued

'Special?'

'She can do things others can't.'

'But she can't speak. Was she born like that?'

Rose shook her head. 'She stopped speaking about a year ago. A year after mum went missing.'

So her muteness wasn't to do with the loss of her mother, it was to do with something else.

'Did she see something traumatic?'

Rose looked unaccountably frightened. She stood up, quickly.

'Night, night, Max,' she said, and before he could say anything to prevent her from leaving, she had gone, shutting the door behind her.

Max lay awake in bed, trying to get to sleep. A knocking started up at his window. Climbing out of bed, he went up to the window, drew open the curtains and looked out. He gasped. Through the glass, a man with heavy-lidded eyes was staring at him. Max gave a violent start and put his hand to his mouth. So did the man. *He was mimicking him*. Max laughed – *it was just his reflection.*

Max put his eye right up to the windowpane to see

through the glass's reflection but could only make out the dark shapes of the topiary hedges. A full moon hung sullenly over the garden.

Leaving the curtains open, Max withdrew from the window into the interior of his room. His reflection turned its face to the left. *But Max had not moved his head.* His reflection then looked around to face him again and smiled. *But Max was not smiling.* And then, slowly, Max watched as his reflection visibly aged in front of him, deep lines growing over his skin like ivy, the form of his face shrinking and drooping like the leaves of a dying plant.

The reflection of an old man stared back at him, his lips opening and whispering so softly Max had to lean forward until his ear was touching the cold, pure glass of the window pane. He could just make out the words, '*Carpe diem,* Max, *carpe diem.*'

CHAPTER 9

JAMES RETURNED FROM London like a force of nature and at supper, that evening, glittered with witty aperçus and long, winding stories. He was on better form than Max had ever seen him. There was a charged charisma about him. Max wondered if it was somehow connected to Rose going out for the evening with Ryan. His eyes sparkled and his patrician manner seemed more lightly worn than usual, as if he could slough it off like a snakeskin, at any moment.

Max wondered how James was getting on with his next novel. Perhaps he had just organised another book deal with the Meerkat. Although all his agent's incisors had been drilled flat for a radiant smile, whenever Max heard the name 'Meerkat', he just thought of the rotting carcasses of dead writers piled up in their burrows for the winter, for the Meerkat babies to nibble on.

Over the cheese and biscuits, the candlelight flickering, James asked, 'What do you think of Rose?'

'She's a lovely girl,' Max said, as if indifferent to her.

'She is. A very special girl.'

Max nodded. James lounged back in his chair in navy chinos and open-necked white shirt like the Great Gatsby. Max wondered how many beautiful silk ties he had lying on his bed. No matter how Max dressed, he looked like either a tramp or an estate agent. No matter how hard he tried, he always managed to feel as if he were coming – literally – undone. His clothes didn't flow the way James's clothes flowed.

With James it wasn't just the style of clothes he chose, it was the way he wore them, as if he had been draped in soft fabric rather than bothering to dress. And he always smelt cut-grass clean. At first, looking at James, you would never have guessed that he had suffered the loss of his wife. But Max noticed that, when James fell silent, a slight weariness entered his eyes, like a thief in the night.

'What do you think of Ryan?' James asked.

Max made a quick calculation and decided it would be more prudent to remain neutral. He didn't want to reveal the jealousy *he* was feeling over Ryan and Rose.

'He seems like an ordinary guy.'

James pounced.

'Exactly. An ordinary guy.' James smiled, the cat who had got the cream. 'You're a very perceptive guy, Max, that's why I like you so much. And the more I get to know you, the more perceptive you seem to get.' He let out a big hearty laugh. He had no fillings, or if he had, they had all been replaced by white ones. 'I don't think ordinary is good enough, though, do you?'

Max privately thought ordinary was bloody, euphorically fantastic. The older he got, the more in awe of ordinary he became. Ordinary was the holy grail. Why, it almost sounded like its anagram.

'You mean good enough for Rose?' Max asked.

'I mean for Rose.'

'Perhaps he grounds her. Keeps her feet on the ground,' Max offered, tentatively.

'That's exactly what he does. When she should be soaring . . .'

'Rose seems to know what she wants,' Max pointed out. Where *was* he getting these platitudes from, he wondered, secretly impressed by them. He didn't know he'd had them in him.

'There's just a stubborn quality about him . . .' James said, trailing off significantly. He stood up. 'Well, Max, as Freud said, all women are a combination of masochism and narcissism. And my darling Rose is no exception.'

He pushed his chair under the table. 'Goodnight, Max. It's good to have you here. Reassuring to have someone to talk to, like this.'

Max remained sitting at the table for a while, in

front of the remnants of their meal, wondering when James would ever offer to help him with his next book. He was still waiting for that moment when James would casually say he would recommend Max to his powerful female editor. That was what was supposed to happen. But Max knew very well that life had a habit of not going where it was supposed to go – actually, more often than not, veering off in exactly the opposite direction. But nonetheless, with the inevitable triumph of hope over experience, Max was certain if he stayed on Burnt Island long enough and didn't make any irrevocable mistakes, a moment would present itself, a moment that would transform his life.

Outside the library, in the centre of the village, the next day, Max bumped into Dr Macdonald. She was wearing heavy dark-rimmed horn glasses and a long beige trench mackintosh. He could see shapely legs encased in shimmering, grey stockings peeping out between the gap in the mackintosh as she walked.

'How are you settling in?' she asked.

'Oh fine,' Max replied. 'James has been very hospitable.'

'That's good.'

She gave an enigmatic smile.

'Has your husband gone back to the oil rig?' he asked. It didn't sound quite right.

'He most certainly has. How's your cut? It looks completely healed now.'

She looked approvingly at his wound-free head.

'Thanks to your expert treatment.'

'You're probably right.'

She was wondrously literal, he thought. The unimaginative were unaffected by possibility or doubt and this made them strong. He supposed doctors believed in direct causal results more than most people. There was no room for manoeuvre or philosophical debate when you were dealing with a malignant disease.

'You looked after James's previous lodger too, didn't you?' Max asked.

'Yes, a very intense young man. Unfortunately, he hadn't been on the island long when he became delusional. And his extreme intelligence made it impossible to reason with him. I gave him a prescription for anti-psychotic drugs but I don't think he ever used it.'

'What kind of delusions?'

'Monsters of some kind. He said they would come out of the sea. Take on human form. That they would follow him. It was always when he felt at his weakest, he said. As if they preyed on his vulnerabilities.'

'And how did they know he was vulnerable. Were they telepathic monsters?'

Dr Macdonald gracefully ignored Max's tone.

'They seemed to sense weakness, yes. He said they could smell his fragility. So he tried not to be vulnerable. To be strong. Not to ruminate or dwell on things. But the more he tried not to, the more he did.'

Max knew madness was only a little side step to the left of imagination. He remembered how after his marriage collapsed he had refused anti-depressants, frightened they might threaten his creativity. He had become attached to his creativity like a hostage to his captor. Sometimes he felt he was trapped in a labyrinth and he was Theseus, the thread and the minotaur, all at the same time.

'He kept saying the monsters were real,' Dr Macdonald continued, 'as real as you or I. And then in the summer, he went missing.'

'Like Natalie?'

'Like Natalie. And on the same day.'

What an unlikely coincidence, he thought.

After he and Dr Macdonald had parted, he looked up at the library. The library was a wooden hall rather than a stone edifice. He opened the door and entered. The librarian, who was sitting behind a table in the middle of the hall reading a book, glanced up when he came in. She had gooseberry eyes, and a strong chin and low forehead, which came together to form an almost monstrous shape, as if various bits of faces had been put together to form a singular one. With a surprisingly lithe, attractive body there was something beguiling about her lack of conventional beauty, like a woman with a beast's head. She seemed furious to see him; this was her domain and he was the intruder.

'I wanted to look at the local newspapers from two years ago,' Max said.

He could tell the more he tried to charm her, the more she would resist. She was the type of woman who would see his charm as a weapon against her, as a way into her dusty, dark archives . . . which it was.

'I'm afraid we don't have a filing system for that.'

'But you do have the actual newspapers?'

She stared at him, as if he had asked for the grilled heart of a baby panda.

'I couldn't tell you. I'm not responsible for management collection,' she said, coldly.

In desperation, he gave it a final shot.

'I'm staying with James Fairfax.'

She finally, if not exactly smiled, looked less grim.

'Oh, well, if that's the case . . . I'm always happy to help any friend of James's.'

She took him to the corner of the hall where newspapers had been loosely filed into boxes. He searched through the papers to find the ones covering the summer of the year Daniel and Natalie had gone missing. Flicking through the July papers, he came upon a news article about Daniel's disappearance. Next to the article was his photograph.

Max stared at Daniel's face, trying to glean some kind of truth from it, as if its physiognomy could hold the answers for him. Daniel's features were so symmetrical they looked like half a face reflected in a mirror. His lips were thin but appeared mobile as if they liked to speak more than kiss, but looking at the serious intentness of his dark eyes, Max conjectured the opposite was probably the case.

There was an intense stillness to his expression that seemed to hide a passionate nature. Passion tended to hide. Passion was infinitely malleable. A contortionist, its properties so dark and secret it could take any shape or form. Passion was not part of the visible, real world. There was always something unreal about passion, Max thought, which made those with imagination so vulnerable to it.

Fantasy upon fantasy built up in the head until desire became a towering Babel of language and dreams. But a tower built on water. With a cage suspended deep below, an archetype that imprisoned lovers behind bars of iron, eroded by rust with the bars not visible because of the darkness of the water.

He read the paragraph on Daniel's short life – single, thirty-two, author of one moderately success-ful, literary novel. His body had never been found, presumed washed out to sea. Reading the newspaper article carefully, it did seem an accidental death; that Daniel, wading into the sea, had been caught out by the tide even though warned about it frequently. The article noted that Natalie Fairfax had disappeared on the same day. But the articles concerning her dis-appearance had been torn out from all the relevant papers.

During the night Max woke up to the sound of a woman screaming, coming from deep within the bowels of the house. Following her cries, he blearily made his way down the stairs but the screams began to slowly fade away. Had it been a strange waking dream? As he returned to his room, he felt oddly aroused and nervous at the same time.

A few minutes later he heard the door of James's bedroom quietly shut. Max crept out of his room again and down to James's room. He could just make out, through a slit, James sitting on the edge of the bed, bending over and groaning, as if in terrible pain.

Max quickly turned away to bump into Esther in the corridor. Her wide, lemur eyes looked up at him.

'Did you hear a woman crying out?' he asked, trying to deflect attention away from his spying on her father.

Whenever he asked Esther a question, she pursed her little lips. She looked as if she had understood the question, wanted to answer it, but the words stopped at the roof of her mouth, just behind her shut lips. She was on a path she couldn't get off, a path made of stony words she kept stumbling over. This little girl was forced to walk the path again and again, without expression or permission. There is so much that is unexpressed in this house, Max thought. All these mysterious events are just an attempt to articulate it.

Esther just shook her head.

CHAPTER 10

OVER THE FOLLOWING days, Max became increasingly sure that James was going to ask him for a favour in return for his lodgings, but he did not know what the favour was, only that it would probably have profound ramifications. He knew it was just a question of time before he would find out what the favour was, whether through James asking him directly or perhaps through a mutual, silent coming-together of minds.

At breakfast one morning, James said, 'You know Max, it's hard sometimes to live with my success!'

Max laughed. 'Don't tell me you're asking for pity!'

James shook his head. 'Not for pity. Just not for jealousy. And other writers are jealous. They think my first novel's success goes against the natural order of things.'

'Don't forget you can take pride in the writing itself.'

James looked at him strangely, *as if he had forgotten he had written* Lifeblood.

'Oh, yes. And that. Of course. That too.'

'But it must mean so much,' Max insisted.

'You know sometimes I feel like I didn't really write it. That someone else did.'

James would never dare say this, Max thought, if he hadn't been the authentic author of *Lifeblood*. This was proof that James was the Real Thing. And Max understood exactly what he meant. Having finished a novel, *he* always felt someone else had written it. He would reread his writing in a condition of mild surprise and curiosity, as if his novel had been nothing to do with him.

He would love to have written a novel, taken a step back, and said, *Yes I wrote that; I claim it as mine.* But as soon as he had finished a novel, it drifted away from him like a book sinking into water, swirling away out of sight into the gloomy depths. Tumbling, falling into darkness, there would be a final gleam as the book fell open to reveal its white pages, and then nothing.

'Were you surprised by its reception?' Max asked.

James looked at him.

'I was, very. It's been a phenomenon. But also a terrible burden. The weight of expectation for my next book is huge. From publishers. From readers. The next book has become like an albatross hanging around my neck.'

'Because it has to be so good?'

'Exactly. And good in the same, quicksilver way. Critically acclaimed. Popular.'

Max knew of other writers – Salinger for instance – who never recovered from the acclaim of their first book. Salinger had wanted to run away from its success. Begin again. And it was never possible to begin again. You could never begin with yourself again. You always had your memories.

'But, hey, I don't want your pity. Here I am, complaining. How self-indulgent. When writers who have written for decades have not had a thousandth of the success I've enjoyed. Writers like you, Max.'

His heart quickened.

'And of course,' James continued, 'I have a great deal of influence ... The right word about you in the right ear ... But first, Max, there's something I'd like you to do for me. A little bit of research.'

'For your next novel?'

'Not exactly. I'd like you to find out more about Ryan.'

'*Ryan?*' Max couldn't keep the incredulity out of his voice.

'I think he may have had something to do with Natalie going missing.'

Max was speechless.

'I just feel he's a little too secretive ...' James

continued, 'and you see he's going out with Rose and Rose is so precious to me. *She's so like Natalie.*'

'But he seems to me such a straightforward guy. A garage mechanic.'

'He's also very good looking. And my wife. She was somewhat younger than I was ...'

'You think there was something between them? Ryan and Natalie?'

'Who knows ...'

'But the mother. Then Rose. Isn't that a bit strange?'

James looked at him as if he were mad. 'Not really. Sometimes I think it would be easy to mistake them *for the same woman.*'

That afternoon, Max visited to the garage to find Ryan stooping over a decrepit car, young, conceited and covered in liquid oil with the sheen of a rainbow. Peter was just coming out of the door of the small office. Peter did a double-take when he saw Max.

'I almost didn't recognise you. You look thinner. How are you getting on?' Peter asked.

'Fine.'

'How's Mr Fairfax?'

'Very hospitable ... Peter?'

'Yes?'

'He's the benefactor, isn't he? Who pays for writers to come over to Burnt Island?'

'Can't tell you that, Max. Sorry,' Peter replied. 'Don't forget – if you ever need me . . .'

Peter left the garage quickly. Max turned to Ryan, who was looking at him with an amused expression on his face.

'What can I do for you?' Ryan asked.

What, on this barren island, this wasteland with grassy dunes and white sands and cypress trees, dark and mysterious like the silhouettes of dreams? Max wanted to ask, but instead found himself saying, 'Rose sends her love.'

Ryan looked surprised, his masculine wide forehead creasing. Max noted for the first time there was a latent passivity about him that contrasted with the coiled-up energy of his muscular body. His full lips and brimming, blue eyes were unpredictably feminine. Max wondered if it was this strange combination of masculine and feminine that had first drawn Rose to him.

'That's not why you've come, is it? To send me Rose's love? I should imagine it's the last thing you'd want to give me,' Ryan said.

'What do you mean?'

'I see the way you look at her. But she's just a flirt.

Like her mother was. Two peas in the same pod. They don't mean anything by it.'

'You knew Natalie?'

'She was always coming round to the garage. To get things fixed. James Fairfax thought there was something between us.'

'And there wasn't?'

'What business is it of yours?' He relented. 'But no. Of course not. That would be seedy, wouldn't it, the mother? Then the daughter?'

'Stranger things have happened,' Max pointed out.

Ryan laughed, a big, hearty laugh.

'In that family, probably yes. But I think Natalie just wanted company. She did seem to like the company of younger men, that's for sure. Men her own age seemed half dead compared to her. Nor did she have much time for the company of women. She said all they wanted to talk about was curtains and cupcakes.'

'What was she like?'

'She seemed to be looking for something.'

'People don't always find what they're looking for,' Max said. In fact, he thought, *more often than not* they don't. As if the looking actively prevented them from finding it.

'And you don't think it odd she just got up and left

James and her daughters? Just abandoned them like that?' Max asked.

'She felt trapped by James. And she felt trapped by Burnt Island.' Ryan wiped his oily hands with a cloth. 'But she'd have found it difficult to settle anywhere. She was never satisfied. But as I said, she was always searching for something that would make her happy.'

'Something like you?'

He shrugged his shoulders. 'I've told you. She was never interested in me in that way. She was just lonely. And she would say she liked me because I talked straight. She always knew where she was with me.'

Unlike being with a writer, Max thought. Max understood the trickiness of writers. It was in their nature. They were like rabbits cowering in their dark earthy holes, playing patience.

'How do you think she got off the island?'

'Probably stowed away on the ferry. Early. Hid.'

'And after she left, she never tried to contact you?'

'From the mainland? No, why should she? I told you there was nothing between us.'

Max couldn't tell whether he was telling the truth. Ryan certainly gave the impression of being direct. If there *was* a sinister motive behind Natalie's disappearance, it was probably sexual and even if Ryan had slept with Natalie, it didn't mean he'd killed her. Just because he was good with his hands . . .

'Were there any clues before she went missing?' Max continued.

'None at all. She seemed her usual self.'

'So you think that's what happened? She just ran away?'

'Must have. Although if people do drown around here, their bodies never come ashore. It's to do with the currents.'

'What was the previous writer like who came on the fellowship?'

'Daniel?'

'He was in the same room I'm staying in. I found his clothes in the wardrobe,' Max said.

'Why are you so interested in him?'

'Oh, you know. Just curious.'

'Well, you know what happened to the cat.' Ryan gave him a big smile.

'It's the writer's occupational hazard.'

'Sure. How's your book going?'

'Oh, coming on fine,' Max lied.

It was always the easiest thing to do, to lie to fend off any awkward explanations – people never understood writer's block. They thought it was something writers could move out of the way like a pile of bricks. They didn't understand it was a *state of mind*. Writer's block was a phrase that struck fear into a writer, no matter how long they had been writing. It could strike at any time, without rhyme or reason, like a crisis of faith, like a religious man finding out there was no God. As if the charade of writing a novel, the audacity of it, was suddenly revealed for what it really was. There was no God. The Novel was dead and talent shows and pornography and war were the only things left in the world.

'What's it about?'

'Sorry?'

'What's your book about?'

'Oh, I don't like to talk about it when I'm actually writing it. Might jinx it.'

'Oh, right.'

Ryan didn't look as if he believed him.

'You're looking pasty,' Ryan said. It was true Max was looking more sallow than usual. He had noticed deeper shadows under his eyes.

Walking back to the house, Max thought about his next book. Perhaps what was happening on Burnt Island had the beginnings of his bestseller. It certainly seemed to have all the makings of a horror plot: a mysterious island, a famous writer, a missing wife, a drowned lodger, a beautiful daughter and a handsome garage mechanic. Why, it was practically a Greek play.

CHAPTER 11

HE WOKE UP suddenly in the night to the sound of the window being blown open by the wind. Shutting the window, he returned to bed, but as he lay there trying to fall asleep, he heard a breathing in his ear, the breathing of an aroused woman, and sensed the lightest trace of her hair against his face. The air was hot, very hot. She seemed to be emanating an intense warmth around her; he could smell the perfume of white jasmine. But Max was unaccountably unable to move.

Who are you? he heard himself ask. He hardly recognised the sound of his own voice. It sounded like the voice of someone who had lost the outer shell of his personality. *You know who I am,* echoed loudly in his head, as if the words had been spoken out loud.

A wave of cold air blasted through his bedroom. It was as if Max had received the body blow he had been waiting for all his life. A wave of inconsolable grief washed over him, a sense of loss too deep for tears. *Come back,* he found himself saying to her – now in his own voice, clear as a bell. *Come back.* Motionless, he lay in bed, waiting.

The window blew open again. He leapt out of bed and banged it shut, hard. Having examined the latch, he decided it was not faulty. Without undoing the latch, he tried to push the window open but it wouldn't budge. His growing unease on the island seemed to have made the window open of its own accord. But these were the thoughts of a deluded man; he had written too many words with which he could create and adjust reality according to his whim.

At dawn, as the lightening sky was turning a muted pink, Max heard the sound of his door quietly opening. He sat up in bed, bleary from lack of sleep, and saw Rose standing in the doorway, the form of her body in its white negligee clearly outlined by the early morning light. Everything about Rose seemed transparent. He could see every inch and crease and fold of her flesh. He wondered how like her mother she was. Natalie had liked men. He wondered if it was genetic, their sensual nature.

'Can I come in?'

'Of course you can.'

But she looked reluctant. She slowly came in and sat down on the edge of his bed.

'What are you up to, Max? I feel there's another reason you're here. Apart from your writing, I mean.'

Max didn't say anything.

'It seems to me, Max,' Rose continued, 'you're like the dog in the Aesop's fable with a bone in his jaw, which he drops for the bone's reflection in the water.' She smiled, then added, 'Don't expect anything from him.'

'What do you mean?'

'Dad is very good at getting people to do things for him. But he never does anything for them in return.'

'He's letting me stay in his house.'

'You want more from him than that, though, don't you? You want him to help you get a publisher for your next novel.'

'I'm not doing anything for him and I'm not expecting anything in return,' Max lied.

'Well, that's very sensible of you.' She took his hand.

'You know,' Rose continued, 'Dad is very charming. And I've always been wary of charm. What are people charming for? Why did they have to learn it? Why can't they just be who they are?'

'I like charm,' he countered. 'It's so rare.'

'So is out-and-out cruelty. Just because it's rare doesn't make it OK.'

'It's better than rudeness.'

'At least rude people can't manipulate you.'

'Your father isn't manipulating me.'

'See, it's working . . . don't you see, what you have is better?'

'What's that?'

'Self-doubt. Sometimes I fear Dad is like the golden goose laying its golden eggs. If someone did kill him and cut him open there would be nothing inside!'

She bent down and kissed him on the mouth. She tasted of silk. He immediately thought of James again. There is something so interconnected about them, he thought. Father and daughter shared the same psychic energy. He could see her full breasts swaying slightly towards him beneath her negligee.

'But you do love him?' he asked.

'Of course I do. I would do anything for him. And I know he feels the same way about me . . . We should go down for breakfast.'

Not long after they'd had breakfast, there was a ring at the door. 'That will be the journalist from *Byline*,' James said to Max. 'Can you fend her off? In a weak moment, I said I'd see her. I did a phone interview with her a few days ago and became so carried away, I agreed to see her in person. I've got to get to London now. Thanks, Max.' And then James, carrying a suitcase, fled the house by the back door.

Standing on the front doorstep was a middle-aged woman, emanating a glossy look of immaculate grooming with her white-blonde hair, fawn-coloured clothes and pitch-black sparkling eyes. Her fine delicate face had been hardened and sculpted, as if by willpower. The shape of her body fitted perfectly into the outline of a schoolgirl except for the tottering, dark, heavy-heeled shoes at the ends of her legs, smooth as carved wood. She flashed him a smile.

'You are James.' She whispered the name as if pronouncing the name of an ancient Egyptian god. 'I am Melissa.'

Max could tell it was Melissa's driving ambition that had given her this detached, robotic manner. He, on the other hand, prided himself on being in the moment. Even if the moment was wracked by self-loathing.

'Unfortunately, I'm not James,' Max explained. 'James had to leave on important business.'

He tried not to take her evident, acute disappointment personally. He offered her coffee and tried to entertain her. Melissa was clever, whiplash, calculatingly clever, and Max was reminded of Dr Hoffman's favourite saying, '*It wasn't poetry but reason that sent me mad.*' He quoted it out loud under his breath, without thinking.

Overhearing the words, Melissa looked at him with such astonishment that he actually saw her retract like a piece of machinery, her arms and legs flinching away and her face averting. It was a strange combination, he thought, ruthless ambition and fastidiousness, but he could intuitively sense a connection.

'So what's your magazine about?' he finally asked.

Max hoped perhaps she would interview him, too, once she found out he was a writer.

'It's an arts magazine. A huge circulation. Over a million,' she replied. 'You're a writer too?'

'Yes. Of seven novels.'

'That's impressive.' But he could see in her dark eyes that it was not.

'Highbrow?' She made it sound like the name of an Eastern delicacy.

'So I've been told.'

'But difficult to sell?'

'Exactly. That's why I'm working on a different kind of book. More accessible. No symbolism. No metaphors. Actually,' he said, getting carried away, 'hardly any words at all.'

She looked at him blankly.

'Pictures?'

'No, I just meant . . .' he trailed off. What *did* he mean? That he hadn't started it yet?

'At least you're working on something! James has writer's block. He's devastated by it.' *So James had writer's block, too.* James had mentioned the pressures of following up on *Lifeblood*'s success. It also explained his empty desk.

'He's told you this?'

Melissa gave a superior smile. 'Not in so many words. But between the lines. In the phone interview I did with him, the other day.'

'Here.' She took out her tape recorder and, after a few minutes' listening to the headphones, found the part of the conversation she'd been looking for. 'Listen to this.'

She took the headphones off and pressed the speaker button on. 'It's like this,' James was saying in his urbane, pleasant drawl, 'I'm rummaging about for a new idea. It's been a while since *Lifeblood* has come out. Too long. But nothing's occurring to me. Agent on my back. But something will turn up. It always does. In fact, *I think something already has.*'

She switched off the recorder.

'Oh, well, it sounds like he's found something to write about,' Max said glibly.

CHAPTER 12

MELISSA LEFT AS quickly as she had come and it was as if she had never been. Nor did James return that evening. As Max passed Esther's room on retiring to bed, he could hear soft murmurings coming from inside. The door was ajar, and, wondering who was talking to her, he peered in.

Rose's profile was clearly silhouetted, as she sat cross-legged in her dressing gown on the floor. Her brown hair fell in soft curls around her shoulders. She was issuing hushed instructions to Esther, who was bending under her bed and bringing out a board. Esther then solemnly placed the yellowing board engraved with faded lettering on the floor between them.

Max watched, as Esther lit some candles and placed them in a circle around the Ouija board. The two girls' faces looked fragile in the candlelight, their skin smooth as if made of yellow wax too, with their eyes glittering like the white stamens of the flames. Esther proceeded to scatter some photographs onto the floor, their images falling into the shadows.

Esther placed a glass tumbler on the centre of the board in the circle of letters and both girls put their fingers on top of the tumbler.

Rose quietly asked, 'Mummy, are you there?'

With the girls' hands lying lightly on the tumbler, it seemed to move of its own accord around the board.

'Yes!' Rose finally announced. 'See, I told you she would be here tonight, Esther.'

Esther nodded vigorously, a big smile on her lips. Max had never seen her look so joyous. It made him feel correspondingly sad that she should believe her mother was speaking to her.

'Are you all right, Mummy?' Rose asked.

A few minutes passed before the tumbler finished spelling out the letters. Esther looked expectantly at Rose, waiting for her to read out loud the words the letters had spelt out.

'BE CAREFUL,' Rose announced, quietly.

Max formed the impression, by their practised manner, that the daughters did this regularly, had a conversation with their missing mother, after tea on a Thursday night. They both clearly believed she had been lured into the sea by Sirens and drowned.

'Oh look, it's happening again!' Rose cried.

The two girls watched, as the tumbler seemed to

move of its own accord across the board. Rose read out loud the words the tumbler spelt out.

'JAMES IS *LO DIABLO*.' Rose went ashen. She knew what *LO DIABLO* meant, but Esther didn't. Esther looked at her sister enquiringly.

'It's Spanish for sad, Esther. Mummy is saying Daddy is sad.'

The next morning, after Rose and Esther had gone downstairs for breakfast, Max quickly slipped into Esther's room. The photographs from the night before were still lying on the floor. He picked some up; they were all pictures of the same woman. In an older photograph there didn't seem to be anything special about her. *She was in shadow*. She had brown hair, pallid skin, dark eyes. But as he looked harder, he could see a haunting in her eyes. She was feline, he thought, slippery, with a nervous, wild unhappiness in her eyes. Her posture was languid.

He looked at a more recent photograph. In this photograph, Natalie's body was poised and alert, as if it had been brought alive, and the sadness in her eyes had been replaced by an expression of joy. Her eyes were now excited and serene at the same time, those flecks of green and brown shot with gold. One photograph had her holding hands with Rose. She and

Rose had a similar expression of intensity that irradiated their faces. They could have been reflections of each other.

The final photograph had been cut in half. A man's arm was around Natalie's shoulder, loose and dangling, casual, the fingers lightly splayed. But the rest of the figure had been cut off. They were both standing under one of the cypress trees.

Looking out of the window, Max saw, once more, the figure in the garden slipping between the trees. The trees loomed dark green and spiky, monstrous figures twisting out into the night sky, like images from an ancient world. In pyjamas and slippers, Max climbed down the shiny, wooden stairs.

Outside, as he walked across the garden, the moonlight cast a pale beam of light over the various shadows and crevices. The dew on the grass seeped through the soft material of his slippers, so it felt as if his feet were bleeding painlessly. His mind was on fire, as when an action takes on what is inadvisable but irresistible.

The garden was brimming with the different abstract shapes of the topiary. Max's dark, curly hair had become matted by the light rain that was gently falling both on the lawn and also on all the things in it – a self-enclosed world with its own laws and meanings. As he walked through the shadows of the topiary, he had the sensation of becoming possessed. His thoughts seemed to be changing into the geometric forms of the topiary, taking on planed outlines beyond his control. But there was no sign of the mysterious figure he had seen.

He reluctantly turned back to the house. Entering the hallway, he bumped into James, who was standing in the entrance as if struck by an idea, his mask-like face still and taut.

'You've come back,' Max said, as if uttering the spell that had summoned up James's presence in the first place.

'I just got back an hour ago. The plane was delayed.'

'Does Rose know?'

'I phoned her from the airport. But you look ill. Are you OK?'

Max nodded vigorously. He did not mention the figure he had seen in the garden. He had a tendency to keep quiet about the things that were most important to him, an inverse quality he had learnt about himself. Like the decay of his marriage, which had happened in silence. He could discuss and analyse the superficial details of his life to his heart's content. But when it came to the nexus of the story he was dumbstruck.

Besides, the figure in the garden had seemed so

personal, so amorphous, to do with himself rather than Burnt Island. How wrong he had been. It had all been about place in the end. It had begun and ended with Burnt Island.

Max and James ate supper together in silence, a travesty of a married couple with unspoken grievances. There seemed to be a different aura about the older man tonight, as if his sensuous, handsome face had developed a disfiguring flaw. As James, after the main course, looked up at him, Max was shocked to find he was looking into terror-stricken eyes.

However, he also felt relieved, relieved to be seeing into the soul of the real James, the James he'd always hoped had lain beneath the irreproachably smooth surface. The James who had written *Lifeblood*. Here, imprinted for the first time on his face, was what made his literary genius explicable. Here was agony writ large, the experience of suffering that had wrought *Lifeblood*.

There was always pain at the heart of the best art. It was a one-word manifesto. It was what forged art. Joy was not creative, it simply existed, within itself for itself. It was pain that reached outwards and inwards, in all directions, *pain needed to communicate itself*. And pain created. Pain wrote words, painted pictures, made music. Art that didn't come from pain was just entertainment. And here, finally, Max could see what he had been looking for all these weeks – the locus of James's art – the pain etched on his face as real as the previously refined configuration of his features.

'Is it Natalie?' Max finally asked, in a low voice.

'It's always about Natalie,' James replied. 'And I'll never be able to forgive myself.'

'For what?'

'For not showing her I loved her. You see, I did love her – that was the irony. She thought I didn't, but I did. However, I also took her for granted. Thought whatever I did, I couldn't lose her love. I thought her love was indelible.'

'You lost her love,' Max said, quietly.

'Carelessly, imperceptibly, over the years,' James continued, 'I kept losing her love. *Because I stopped caring*. She would cry and I saw those tears as irritating and demanding as those of a spoilt child. She was trying to save our marriage and I ignored her. In the end she cried so much she smelt of tears. And I just thought it was the perfume of the sea.'

He put his hand on the table, his wedding ring and the signet ring next to it glittering in the candlelight.

'You know, don't you, Max, writers keep falling in

love with that reflection in the water? The writer's so involved with his reflection, he loses track of reality. But in the end reality is all we've got. Reality is what's precious.'

'So you think she left you?'

'Those prosaic words. Yes. *She left me*. Two years ago. I've no idea where. She packed her bags and left. Me. Esther. Rose. Cruel, don't you think? Very cruel.'

At this point, tears were running down James's face.

'What was she like?' Max asked. It never occurred to him it was none of his business what had happened to Natalie. As a writer everything was his business – the entire universe was his business. James looked up, his eyes flickering. James's eyes matched the colour of the sea, varying like the sea according to the light. Max noticed a deep scratch on his neck and what looked like a bruise from a love bite.

'She was like . . . what was she like? She left traces of herself wherever she went.'

'But leaving Rose and Esther too . . .' Max exclaimed.

James took out a handkerchief to wipe away his tears. 'I know it's difficult to believe. But in the end she saw our daughters as an expression of me. She therefore had to reject them too. Her logic was irrefutable.'

'And wrong in the end.'

James looked at Max – was that *gratitude* Max saw in his eyes, gratitude that he understood?

'Exactly. Wrong too. You know where logic can lead to. If the premises are wrong.'

'And the premises were wrong?'

'Of course they were. I loved her but I couldn't get her to believe it.'

'You've no idea where she is now?'

'No idea. But you know, Max, really, *the truth about this island*?' His mood, with an abruptness that was disconcerting, had shifted back to the confident *paterfamilias*.

Max shook his head.

'All the women on this island are demons. Be careful of them.'

And he hurled back his head and laughed, a loud irrepressible laugh like the roar of a giant.

'What do you mean?'

'Well, what do you think of, when you use the word demon?'

'I mean witch-like. Possessed by the devil. Evil.'

'Well, that's what I mean too . . . Rose. Dr Macdonald. The librarian – how I had to work on *her* . . . All of them. Even my Natalie.'

Max couldn't believe what he was hearing; it sounded insane. Ever since Max had first set foot on

Burnt Island it had seemed to him a unique place, a place unlike any he'd been to before.

'Once they have sex with you, they can get you to do whatever they want.'

'I'll be careful, then.'

He laughed again.

'Careful? Careful? You'll have to be much more than that!'

CHAPTER 13

MAX CAME DOWNSTAIRS for breakfast to find Esther sitting at the table, expertly cutting the top off a boiled egg with a flick of her breakfast knife. She looked very focused, her lower lip slightly twisted in concentration. The top fell off to reveal a perfectly melted, golden yolk.

She looked up.

'Hi, Esther.'

She took up the blackboard that was lying in front of her on the table.

What are you doing today? she wrote in chalk on her board.

'I'm going to the village.'

Shouldn't you be writing your book? she wrote down and then underlined 'book' three times.

Esther's muteness seemed normal here. The family had adapted to it. They did not try to get her to speak. It was just accepted that Esther never spoke. It was often the case, he thought, that strange, out-of-the-ordinary signs became incorporated into our daily lives, and we accepted them as if they were nothing odd, when really they were meaningful, rubric omens that we should make the effort to read.

'I'm looking for inspiration on the island; it's not just about hard graft,' he explained.

As he spoke, he felt caught out in a lie within a lie like interweaving branches of a wicker cage he had constructed around himself. For hadn't he promised himself that his next book would not rely on inspiration at all, that his bestseller would be calculated, foreseen, mapped out, and would involve *nothing but* hard graft.

Burnt Island is not for beginners, she wrote.

'What do you mean?'

He felt disconcerted this young girl had so much knowledge about the island.

It does things to people living here. They change.

Esther had a preternaturally ancient manner. Her perception of the world seemed reptilian as she stared at him, through slow, blinking eyes.

I hear you visited Ryan. I don't think you should visit him again. He treats Rose badly.

Max was surprised

'In what way?'

I hear her crying in her bedroom. It wouldn't surprise me if he hits her sometimes.

Why did he get the impression she was lying about Ryan? Why would she be trying to deceive him about such a serious matter? He felt she was lying about Ryan to distract him from the truth. But if Ryan wasn't hurting Rose, who was? He remembered the screams.

'Esther, you shouldn't make accusations about things you know nothing about.'

Will be good for your book, if nothing else.

'I certainly don't intend to write about other people's misery.'

People make a fortune from it.

Max thought of all the misery memoirs that filled the bookshops of the Western world. All that pain shimmering just below the surface, like silver fish.

'Have you ever seen bruises on her? Or cuts?' he asked

Esther thought for a moment.

I've seen red marks on her back.

Max remembered them too. He decided to change the subject.

'Don't you have any friends you can play with?'

No, Daddy won't let me bring them home.

'Why not?'

He doesn't want them to find the room.

'What room?'

She shrugged her shoulders. Her eyes were filling with tears and she was starting to tremble.

'Esther, why won't you speak? *What have you seen?*' But she just stared at him.

Esther had nothing but the swirling of unspoken words in her head like leaves in the wind. She stood up to leave. But not before he heard her saying *Be careful* out loud in his mind.

He returned to his room and took out some paper. A horror story needed just one layer of reality. But he couldn't help feeling some ambiguity was required, something beyond the prosaic. He was frightened of becoming a one-dimensional author creating a flat universe of words. But *no*, he must stop this, must keep to his original plan. *No symbols*. His book must be linear, he must keep the prose transparent, remain true to his purpose. He must not be distracted by his wild imagination, and his fancy ideas, that were drawing him insidiously into woods full of arcane branches silhouetted against the backdrop of a thin, bone-white sky.

He drew an arrow; this is what all bestseller writers did, the Meerkat had told him, they drew diagrams, made little clever squiggles on Post-it Notes, made their ideas of the future real before it had dared to happen.

Rose + Esther → James
Natalie → Ryan + Daniel

Then he wrote, *Strange figure outside James's house.*
Then he crossed it out – too fantastical, too dark and,
worst of all, too obscure. He made a list of names and
wrote descriptions beside each.

Natalie = fickle, unpredictable, unhappy – English
  Madame Bovary
Ryan = dark horse?
Rose = sensual, vulnerable (writer)
Esther = prodigy, traumatised
Daniel = susceptible, intense (writer)
James = successful literary novelist

He then added *Max Long* to the list. Then simply
added: *(writer)*. Then, he scored it out. It was irritating when authors put themselves into books, and
bestseller writers never did that. The veneer of illusion was polished and as absolute as the beginning
of time. He looked down again at the list of names.
The people whom he'd met on Burnt Island.

We writers are like vampires, he thought, living
off the blood of real people. Without the reality our
imagination feeds on, we would starve to death. He

wondered about the real life James's first novel had fed on. Had it drunk down life – liquid and red – deep into the bowels of its text? Might the text of *Lifeblood* contain a clue to Natalie's disappearance?

He searched the rows of bookshelves on the mezzanine balcony for a copy of *Lifeblood* but there was not a single copy. The only trace of James's novel he could find was a framed poster on the living room wall of the cover of *Lifeblood*'s American edition. The black and white poster depicted an attractive couple (clearly models), who were trapped in a cave by an encroaching tide. A line from *Time* magazine was printed in italics beneath.

'A heart-rending portrait of a love affair between a younger man and an older woman written in sensuous prose.'

Max had had only one review from a major paper in his entire writing career. The dictatorial intelligence that had dissected his second novel like a laboratory mouse had driven Max to cold thoughts involving an elderly male critic and green shoots of freshly growing bamboo. Max's train of thought was derailed by a terrible shriek. His heart stopped for a second in the soft, heavy silence that followed. For a moment he couldn't tell the difference between the silence and the cessation of his beating heart.

CHAPTER 14

AGAINST THE BACKDROP of a hot summer sky, the still and silent atmosphere of the dunes seemed to consume him. Even the seagulls had flown high up into the rays of the sun. As Max took off his jacket, he thought he could hear, through the iridescent heat, the sound of distant humming. Inexplicably excited, he followed the sound to the bottom of a high dune and turned the corner to a flat area of grass surrounded by gorse bushes. The humming was growing louder. But he could see no one. Nothing stirred. The bushes, the grass, the little pink thyme flowers, all soaked up the warmth. And Max stood there, soaking up the warmth, too. The humming stopped abruptly, and the silence that followed seemed full of apprehension.

'*Are you all right?*' he shouted out into the still, summer air but there was no reply. If anyone had heard him they would think he was shouting out into the empty air. A few moments later, Rose appeared in the deep dip between the dunes.

'It's *you*,' he said, feeling strangely relieved.

She was wearing a floral dress, dotted with pink

and white sweet peas, pretty and folded in on themselves, delicate as butterfly wings. But underneath her floral exterior, he could sense her resilient intelligence; a wolf festooned with flowers, he thought. He also wondered if flowers disguised not only a shrewd mind but also a lascivious appetite. He could imagine her licking – with a lupine tongue – salty drips from her fragile chin.

'I've been looking for you,' she said.

'Any reason?' he asked.

'There's always a reason,' she replied.

She came right up to him, her face voracious. She smelt of lavender, purple and pungent. He could see now that her skin was made of anemones and narcissi and her hair of peony petals. She was whispering words – *what were the words? He couldn't make them out* – in his left ear. He couldn't tell if it was her or him who felt so unbreakable. They lay down in the dunes together.

His heart was racing afterwards. He could feel hers too, at the same time, and she quickly pulled away from him. She put up a hand to his face and stroked his cheek lightly, as if she were leaving a line of chalk dust on his skin. Her face was as smooth as a seashell and the creases that appeared on it when she smiled reminded him of the lines in the sand. But he felt bewildered: this didn't happen in real life, especially not to him, not now. Rose took out a cigarette.

'Can I have a puff?' he asked.

'I didn't know you smoked.'

'I don't.'

The taste of the smoke was acrid, like his first and only cigarette as a teenager. He felt high and dizzy with one inhalation. He gave it back to her. Her hair was tangled.

'That was the best sex I've ever had,' Max said.

She gave a smile. 'You know why, don't you?'

'I'm too modest to say.'

'No, you idiot. It's because it was the best sex *I've* ever had. It's chemistry.' She laughed.

It *was* chemistry, he thought. You can't argue with chemistry. In the end it came down to the smells and genetic make-up of two bodies. How much it was to do with the look in the eyes, he didn't know. It certainly complicated things. Max grasped her and couldn't let her go. He didn't want to let her go. Even though she was already in his arms, she was sticking to his imagination like candyfloss. She gently extricated herself and he watched her body slowly vanish into her dress like a bee into a flower.

'Don't tell Dad,' she said.

She kissed him lightly on the lips. Her face, bruised

with desire, seemed suddenly tired. Her face darkened
with suspicion of him. Was that how relationships
between men and women ended up – black, mutual
distrust painted over white with desire? Then she
walked down the beach away from him, disappearing
into a dot.

Bewildered, Max waited a while before following her
back in the direction of the house. He was so lost in
thought, he almost missed the cave he'd first noticed
when he'd arrived on the island by boat. From the
beach, the entrance to the cave was only visible when
you were standing directly opposite it, its gaping
hole opening up, like an optical illusion in a painting.
Looking into the cave you could see clearly the grey
hewn rock, but as the interior disappeared into blackness, it was impossible to see how far back the cave
went.

Suddenly, Max felt the sand begin to slither
beneath his feet. Looking down, he could see the sand
shifting. A snake or giant worm seemed to be moving
beneath the surface of the beach. At first he thought
it was a trick of the light. Max involuntarily took a few
steps backwards.

Wind howled in his ear and all around him, whip-
ping the sand up into a looming abstract shape, while

the sea stayed calm. This was not his imagination, he thought, this was *real life*. Real life, visceral, and unpredictable. The sandstorm was engulfing him, blinding him, choking him, as its natural force threatened to bring him to his knees. *I am going to suffocate beneath its weight*, he realised.

And then, as quickly as the sandstorm had appeared, it cleared to reveal a blue summer's day. But the sand had become treacherous. As Max continued his walk home, his feet sank cautiously down into it. Now, when he looked at the world, only a brittle pane of glass seemed to separate his imagination from reality.

As he entered the house, he found himself shaking, his skin severely grazed by the combination of sand and wind, his eyes stinging as if rubbed raw with salt. Sand had infiltrated his clothes. Sand had got everywhere. And running upstairs to the bathroom, he turned on the hot shower with its huge head the size of a tinderbox dog's eyes, and felt the hot water pouring over his naked body, cleansing the sand from his body and mind.

CHAPTER 15

HE REMEMBERED DRIVING to pick up Dot in his car, rackety but with four wheels and a reliable engine. She had a neat fair bob and blue eyes and a tanned self-contained body in a summer dress of checked gingham yellow like daffodil pollen. They had driven through the summer evening, silent and young and excited. When he had kissed her dry lips and she had held him and they had looked at each other, there had been no distance between them at all. Her skin was fresh and he had thought he'd found salvation in her, found dry land.

Everything that was tenuous and fragile in that evening became concrete in the curves and dipping lines of her solid body. He had loved her certainty, the physical certainty of her flesh and hard instruments of bone. She had a slim shape, he couldn't help but notice, that was like a wonderfully constructed story, that always followed a straight line. Her petite, dynamic form was like a novella. To continue the simile, her compact, athletic body was without padding.

'*So you compared her to a book?*' Dr Hoffman had asked, in one of their final sessions.

She had seemed *there*, impossibly present like a hologram of herself, colourful and shadowy and promising reality, at the same time as withholding it from him. Looking back he realised that any emotion that night had come not from her, but from the rose-scented summer evening, writhing and suggestive, all gossamer and piercing birdsong, and he had confused her with the fading light.

Her straight nose, her soft lips and dark blue eyes, her breasts the shape of conical tears, had seemed to offer up to him everything he needed. But this sensual love did not last, turning into a fine pollen mist of feelings that blew away on the wind.

Dot's lack of imagination made her unassailable and indefatigable and gave her a sense of self-worth as sturdy as a stone folly. He had fallen in love with her intransigent sense of who she was. He little realised how quickly her practicality would wear him away. How quickly she would start to find his wayward imagination and indestructible commitment to his work so alienating.

What at first had impressed her about him, his urgent creativity, quickly metamorphosed into what irritated her: the opposite of alchemy. It was only after

childbirth, the demands of a baby, the infernal prox-
imity of conflicting desires, that Max came to wonder
at the extent of his own selfishness.

His love for Dot and Luke went in on itself. He had
begun to live his life through the pages of his novels
and as the later novels became more and more surreal
he withdrew from the domestic scenes that were constructed around him like cardboard stage sets. When
Dot and Luke had left, they were not leaving him, but
the novels he had begun to inhabit. Now he was on
Burnt Island, he could see for himself how his selfishness had stretched out in every direction like the dark,
flat sea.

Burnt Island was slowly eroding who he was, grey
rather than black, insidious rather than petrifying; the
effect of the island on Max had begun as a dulling of
senses and a gradual suspension of sensibilities. Alone
in the house one afternoon, and desperate to find some
inspiration for his new novel, he decided try James's
study again. This time a notebook, identical to the one
he had abandoned in the dunes to the seagulls, lay on
James's desk. Max opened it up.

Inside the notebook were listed the names of the
inhabitants of Burnt Island with just a few perceptive
attributes appended to each character. Next to Max's

name had been written: *possible protagonist?* There was no body of text. Was this James's way of dealing with his writer's block? Using Burnt Island for his premise, just as Max was doing? Then a thought struck Max – had James perhaps stolen into *his* room and was now copying *him*?

Max checked all the drawers of James's desk. Tucked away in the left-hand bottom drawer was a thick, handwritten manuscript on yellowing paper entitled *The Song of Imagination* by Daniel Levy. Max slipped out the first page from the bundle of loose sheets.

> *'She's volatile like the sea. She scares and arouses me in equal measure. Perhaps that's the point of her. Of me. The sea had called out to her. She heard the singing. I can hear it too.' That was how he described her and her story.*
>
> *Most intelligent people, men and women alike, had developed carapaces of irony and judgement that had hardened their smiles and narrowed their eyes. But she had a quality about her that was invisible and evasive like the rushing of wind through a field of grass. A vagueness about her features that refused to be circumscribed. She was more like an imprint of a dream. Diffuse colour*

and light, she had a gleam in her eyes, a dancing irrevocable star shape that refused to give specificity to who she was. It was her mind that seemed to give her distinction in spite of the intangibility of her face and body. It was only on meeting her again and again was he to learn how real her face and body were, and the details of her physicality formed in his mind like the marks of an ice pick on a block of ice, each line giving formation and meaning to what was once transparent.

He would learn that her red lips could sometimes be chapped, that her face was oval and the skin under her eyes was bruised. That her eyes were green one day, dark brown the next and gold at night. And her hair was the brown of a dull worthy country mouse until the sun caught hold of it and turned it a fiery burnished bronze. He would learn that her breasts were tender, the nipples pale pink and her labia densest rose.

He couldn't argue with her presence in the way he could argue with the presence of younger women. She was tender and wise, full of pain and joy in equal measure. He could see on her, like a shadow falling across a forest, time passing. She had trusted him with her pain, like a precious stone she had given him. He felt he had to carry it on her

*behalf. And he wanted to give the pain back to her
and to say have your pain back, it connects me too
greatly to you, I can't carry it. I have pain of my
own. He crouched like a toad beneath a rock, with
this precious stone now shining in his forehead.*

Max knew enough about writing to guess that
although it was a novel, it was intensely autobiograph-
ical. He quickly skim-read the rest of the pages – it was
the story of a love affair between a younger man and
an older woman. The ending was unfinished. But Max
felt he had read the writing somewhere before, like a
dream he could almost but not quite remember. But
how could he have read it? This was an unpublished
first draft by a man who had drowned soon afterwards.

Over the next few days, Max's mind seemed
strangely empty of thoughts except for a slight
humming, in the background, of a tune he vaguely
recognised but could not put a name to. It was as if
reading Daniel's words had somehow exhausted his
mind of all possibilities except for the fact he had read
them somewhere before. The high tone of Daniel's
draft haunted him like a fiendish dream.

Back in his room, Max pulled out his notes. He added
further minor details to his characters down to the size

of their shoe. You never knew when you might need to know the size of your character's foot. One of their shoes could be washed up on the beach. Every detail was like a knife-nick to the edge of his serrated heart. He always used to write his first draft from a sense of endless possibilities, but this was how he had to write now. He had to be self-determined, fully conscious at every stage of the writing; nothing could be accidental.

CHAPTER 16

MAX WAS READING in the living room. For the first time since his arrival on Burnt Island, he could hear James typing in his study above. There was a knock on the front door. Max went to open it. Standing at the door was a short rotund man with a very narrow pointed face. As he approached Max, to shake his hand, Max saw how daintily and quickly he moved, like an elephant in pointe ballet shoes. As he did so, he looked Max up and down, obviously trying to appraise by his clothes what kind of man he was. But one of the advantages of living in the literary world was that you could look scruffy and still be taken seriously.

'And you are one of James's . . .' the visitor hesitated, '. . . one of James's friends?'

'No, I'm Max. Max Long. You're my agent.'

Max, at that moment, hated the Meerkat almost as much as the anonymous sound of his own name.

'I'm staying with James. Helping him out,' Max explained.

'*Max*, of course, I'm so sorry. I didn't recognise

you. You've lost weight. And a bit of hair loss? But, now you're smiling, of course I recognise you!'

For Max was, indeed, trying to smile.

He let him in, feeling like a housekeeper, and shouted up to James. The typing continued for a few minutes, sounding even more insistent. Then James emerged onto the landing, a slightly blank look on his face as if still dripping with the sea of words he had been immersed in. He had on a scarlet silk dressing gown in spite of it being mid-afternoon. His fingers were stained black with ink. He looked like an actor pretending to be a writer and Max felt for a moment as if they were all performing in a dramatic production: the literary writer, the agent and him.

'*Lance*, Lance. Great to see you. Hold on,' James cried.

James came down the stairs, shrugging off his gown to reveal slacks and shirt underneath, and put his arm round Lance, smiling at Max, as if to say, *What else can I do? He's my agent.*

'Don't let us interrupt your busy day, Max,' James said, disappearing with Lance back up the stairs to his study. Max sat down in the living room. First of all he heard laughter and talking but quickly the voices grew louder. And then the shouting began. It was James: 'You have to be patient, Lance. Where's your fucking patience? I'm not churning out French fries.

'Have you any idea who you're talking to? And you're asking me *to get a move on*? What kind of hackneyed phrase is that? You have as much poetry in your soul as a baboon has up his arse. Have you any idea what it's like to have writer's block? There's nothing more terrifying than a blank page. Worse than any monster. The loss of imagination. A page as white as Ahab's whale.

'And you have the nerve to tell me to *get a move on.* As if I was doing the hokey cokey. One foot in, one foot out. My imagination's my life. My lifeblood. It's my kudos, my whole identity. And here you are *chivvying me along.*' He paused for breath and then started up again. 'Actually, you're like a vampire. All of you. You, the agents, the publishers, the booksellers, who feed off my imagination. Trapped inside your dark suits or Jaeger shirtdresses and winning ways – until the moment you bare your victim's neck.

'Don't tell me then, Lance, to get a move on. Don't ever say that to me again.'

James's voice finally petered out, his throat having grown hoarse with his dramatic monologue. Max hadn't heard Lance utter a word. Having made no attempt to interrupt, Lance had waited for James to finish his tantrum and – as most who worked with certain writers learnt to do – acted as if he was really dealing with a naughty child wearing the grown-up clothes it had found in the dressing-up box.

'James, please. I didn't intend to upset you. Really.' Max – attuned to this over the decades – could hear the mollifying tone in Lance's voice assigned to dealing with upset writers. It was the same voice Lance had once used with him.

'It was thoughtless of me,' Lance continued. 'Of course you have to go at your own pace. It's just because of your reputation. We are all so eager to see your next book. But I was being tactless. Extremely tactless. Of course I understand you can't hurry these things. A writer like you can't just switch it on when they want to! It's just I'm champing at the bit to read your next book!'

There was silence. Then James spoke softly, with a cracked voice.

'I'm sorry, Lance, I blew up like that. It's just the stress, you know. So many people are relying on me.'

'Of course.'

'You've no idea what it's like. We writers . . . It's what drives us all insane. Or to drink.'

Listening to him it was easy to forget, Max thought, that James had only taken up writing a few years ago.

Most of his life he had worked as a banker. It was strange to hear him speak like a seasoned pro.

The study door opened and the two men came back down the stairs, James looking ebullient and crest-fallen at the same time, as big men do, Lance's hair flattened by James's outburst and his cute face drawn, but his rotund body still managing to move with preci-sion. Lance managed a nod at Max, as he left the house.

Max decided to run after Lance to see if his agent could spare some time to discuss his own career. He had just reached the village pub when a young man came out of the door. He was handsome and finely moulded, with cat-like green eyes. Lance emerged from the pub a moment later, and stood in the entrance, not noticing Max, who had retreated into the shadows.

Lance was staring at the young man's retreating back with a focused look that had turned his body to stone; it was the look of desire. Max was always amazed by the physical manifestation of thought that desire wrought. It was alchemy, he thought, we were living alchemical creatures. We should go around with our eyes wide open at the wonder of us.

Lance followed the young man up the narrow street, changing the pace of his walking to match the rhythm of the young man's languorous gait. He kept a certain distance behind the young man, as Max did with Lance, each shadowing the other. Gripped by curiosity, Max didn't think about what he was doing. He was acting instinctively. He watched, as Lance took a pen from his pocket and ran up to the young man, who turned to him. Lance handed the pen over to him with a smile, as if to say, *Have you dropped this?*

The young man took the pen silently, and the two men fell into step beside each other as they continued to walk up the street in the direction of the dunes. Max followed them for half a mile until they disappeared into a deep hollow in the grassy dunes. Max peered over the edge, to see the two men embrace and begin to kiss intently.

He was about to turn away, when he saw Lance's head dart violently down, over the young man's neck. A few moments later, Lance lifted his head to look up in Max's direction, blood dripping from his lips, his eyes on fire. Horrified, Max turned and ran towards the house. *I haven't seen what I have just seen,* he said over and over to himself, until he convinced himself it had been a waking dream.

CHAPTER 17

AT DINNER THAT evening, James seemed perturbed. Something was not quite right. He was withdrawn and couldn't stop fiddling with his fork. James had that Zen-like art of saying the right thing at the right time, never putting a word out of place, but this time he asked, almost brusquely, 'How's the research getting on, Max?'

'You know, James,' Max replied, 'I don't think Ryan had anything to do with Natalie going missing. Nor do I think he had an affair with her.'

James looked at him, contemptuously. 'Do you not think I knew that, all along?'

Max was bewildered. 'So why did you ask me to find out about him?'

'I told you. *Rose is precious to me.*'

There was a strange glassiness in his eyes as he spoke. As if he was objectively appraising Max, from a distance. Max felt James was not sitting opposite him at the dinner table but on a rock far out to sea and looking at him through a telescope. He felt doused in sea water. It was a gaze he had never seen before and one that completely undermined his filial feelings for him. For James had become like a father figure to him. Become someone who could perhaps help him in ways his own father had woefully failed to, perhaps fill the hole his father had left in Max's heart. A hole that fitted the silhouette of James perfectly, with his metaphorical silk ties, expensive shirts and expansive manner ingrained by worldly success. But now this look James was giving him, so watchful and defiantly cold.

'Ryan has no head for heights,' James continued. 'I often think it must be quite dangerous for him to go near the edges of cliffs. I'm always warning him not to go so near the edge.'

James seemed to be acting more like a jealous lover than Rose's father. What was he suggesting? Max imagined standing next to Ryan at the edge of a cliff. Yes, there was a drop. Somehow Ryan would slip. And Max would look down – just for a moment – at the small smashed figure lying on the rocks below, like a little doll with its stuffing spilt. He imagined the possible consequences of Ryan falling: marriage to Rose, James's personal promotion of his work.

However, Max's position by default was always inaction. He only came alive on the page, where he acted and felt and loved. Besides, he didn't really think James was suggesting he push Ryan over a cliff. He was being over-suggestible.

'I don't have a head for heights, either,' Max said.

'That's a pity,' James said, 'a real pity.'

The island seemed to take on a sunnier disposition towards Max, as he strode over the undulating dunes the next day, trying to think of a plot for his novel. However, as he reached the beach and started walking along the sand, the smell of a dead animal permeated the air. He followed the smell down the beach to behind a rock. There, half-submerged in a rock pool full of tiny shrimps, anemones and seaweed, lay the naked body of a woman.

The body seemed out of tune with reality, a discordant harsh note. She was face downwards in the water. He could feel the sweat beading like hot pearls on his forehead and forming around his neck like a choker, as he turned the body over. Rose's eyes were shut and her rosebud mouth slightly parted. He touched her stone face.

Max knelt down beside her body for a moment, and felt the damp sand cold beneath him. He then rose unsteadily to his feet, and looked out over the wide desert of sea. He started to run over the heavy, thudding sand, over the prickly grass that scratched his legs, avoiding the treacherous holes of the rabbit burrows concealed in the curves of the dunes.

Running through the village, he could have sworn he saw Rose talking to Peter in the street. But he ignored the evidence of his own eyes and burst into Dr Macdonald's surgery, where she was sitting behind her desk talking to an elderly man about a skin rash. Her hair was pulled up in a bun, every hair slicked unnaturally back – never had it looked so tightly tied up, so controlled.

'What is it, Max?'

'It's Rose,' he said breathlessly. 'I've found her lying dead on the beach.'

A look of incredulity spread over her face, swiftly replaced by a look of concern *as if she thought he had gone mad.*

'But I saw her in the street a few minutes ago, Max. She looked perfectly alive then. Walking and talking and everything.'

'I thought I saw her in the street too. But I've also just seen her dead on the beach.'

'Max, you don't look well. You look like you've seen a ghost. Sit down.'

'I don't look well because *Rose is dead*. That's why I don't look well.'

Dr Macdonald ushered the elderly patient out with a professional air.

'OK, Max. Show me.'

He led her out of the village, over the dunes to the rock pool where Rose had been lying. The rock pool was now empty.

'Someone's moved the body,' he said.

'We're not in the middle of an Agatha Christie novel,' Dr Macdonald said severely in her most doctorly tone. 'Look, let's go around to James's house and see if we can find Rose. Perhaps they've put her body there.'

Her sarcasm enraged Max. For a reserved man he was feeling furious, murderous even. As they walked around to James's house on the peninsula, the doctor said, 'You know, Max, are you sure Burnt Island is the right place for you?'

'What do you mean?'

'It can get isolated here.'

'Are you saying I'm seeing things?'

'No,' she said.

He had fallen into her trap. She was right, she hadn't said it. Not in so many words. She had just got him to say it instead.

'Asylums are for the insane. I'm *not* insane.' But his words echoed weakly in the air.

'Who said anything about asylums?' she replied.

He should shut up. Why was he sounding so defensive? For all his creativity and passion, he had never lost his mind. Yet these irrational things seemed to be happening to him on Burnt Island.

Is that when you lose your mind, when your imagination becomes real and there is no division between what you imagine and what you see? Was that what the island did? Make his dreams come true?

They passed the cypress trees behind which the beautiful glass and steel structure of James's house stood, an icy monument to light and line that arched into the sky like a question mark. Max felt reassured to see it. The house seemed to be the only unchanging thing on the island, although the reflection in its glass changed depth and tone according to the movement and colours of the sky.

He entered through the back door that was always left open. He heard singing coming from the kitchen and the smell of baking bread and ground coffee. It sounded very much like Rose's voice singing 'La Mer'. Relief flooded him. He felt like crying. He went into the kitchen. There she was, standing at the table, her chestnut hair falling down her back.

'Rose!'

She turned around. It *was* Rose, smiling with those steely eyes.

Dr Macdonald followed him into the kitchen.

'Why, hello, Rose. You've a nice singing voice.'

Rose smiled, clearly waiting for Dr Macdonald to explain her presence. Max gave her a pleading stare not to elucidate.

'Max has kindly offered to give me a tour of the garden.'

'Oh, of course. I won't come with you, though. I'm afraid flowers don't really interest me.'

For a moment, Dr Macdonald and Max gazed at her floral-print dress and the cloth daisies in her hair. Rose was not interested in real flowers, was what she meant. She just liked the representations. He took Dr Macdonald into the garden. Her horn-rimmed glasses glimmered in the sunlight.

'Thank you, Dr Macdonald.'

'For what?'

'For not saying anything. I suppose it's patient confidentiality and all that.'

'No, Max, it's not that.'

A red admiral butterfly fluttered amongst the hollyhocks.

'I can't explain it all,' Max found himself saying.

'Perhaps you'd been dreaming.'

Perhaps it *had* been another strange hallucination. They could see from the garden Rose in the kitchen, ingenuous and real, baking bread, her white arms made whiter by the flour sticking to her skin. They started to walk back towards the surgery.

'Imagination is a terrible thing, Max. It perverts reality. You can lose yourself in it. Not realise what's really happening to you. Rather than "life is what happens when you're making plans" for you it should be "life is what happens when you're making up stories"!

'You think what you see is real life. But is it? How do you know? Do you know what Rose is really like? James? What Rose is really doing behind your back? After Natalie and Daniel vanished, James and Rose suddenly became very close. It was as if she had willingly taken her mother's place.' She paused and then continued. 'The thing about Natalie was that she had a directness that saw through the flummery of life. I often wondered what she was doing with James.'

'What do you mean?'

'Haven't you noticed? He's an actor. He's always saying his lines. Strutting about the stage. I think Natalie only gradually realised that he was a chameleon. That what she had fallen in love with wasn't real. She was living a charade. Which for Natalie would have been unbearable. She would have felt as insubstantial as a gossamer wing.'

'Why are you telling me all this?'

He followed her into her surgery.

'I'm trying to tell you to get off the island before it's too late. It was too late for Daniel.'

'What I don't understand is how you know so much about it all?'

She reached over to a bookshelf and took out a book and gave it to him.

'I think you should read this.'

He looked down at the book; it was a copy of *Life-blood*.

'I've already read it.'

'I think you should reread it. You've clearly forgotten all the words.'

Dr Macdonald then suddenly turned towards him. To his horror, her face had become livid. Her eyes were glittering and her lips slack. Saliva bubbled at the corner of her mouth. Her body looked even more angular than normal, as if people had inserted steel wire into her limbs.

'You have so much talent, Max. Don't waste it here.'

'But my fellowship!'

'Haven't you realised it's just a ruse James uses? To get writers onto the island.'

'James is the benefactor?'

'Of course, who else could it have been?'

He saw that her hands were clenched like claws.

'Get out of here,' she hissed, 'now.'

His heart was beating hard with fear and confusion. He could hardly believe what he was seeing. As he turned he saw through the open door of the adjoining room at the back of the surgery two hooded figures hunched over a table. A naked young man was lying on it. Max was sure he saw the glitter of a blade in one of their hands. Dr Macdonald slammed the door quickly. Her face had relaxed but as she turned around he saw that her hands were bruised and the nails engrained with blood.

'Have you got anything for these dreams? These waking hallucinations? They seem so real,' he asked desperately.

'Here, take these.' She suddenly seemed normal again and she gave him a bottle full of tiny white pills, pale as chalk.

'What do they do?

'They will stop the dreams.'

He took two that evening before he went to bed.

CHAPTER 18

THE ISLAND WAS becoming increasingly oppressive
and the rustling beauty-sensation of the cypress trees
seemed to be whispering threatening words. The still
sky that had once been serene had become static, as
if about to crack or split in two. The life-giving sea,
teeming with possibility, was now washing up intima-
tions of death onto the shore.

He bumped into Ryan in the street. 'Nice morning,'
Ryan said to him. Then Max bumped into Dr Macdonald. 'Nice morning,' she said. There was an inflexion
in her voice that echoed exactly the rhythm of Ryan's
words. He formed the definite impression they were
somehow both in it together. Whatever *it* was.

Some evil lurked on Burnt Island but he couldn't
work out where the malignancy lay. The troubling
aspect of the island was evasive, amorphous, creeping
up behind him only to vanish when he turned around.
But he was also aware that his sense of the inhabitants'
complicity chimed with his natural paranoia.

'Max!' he heard behind him. He turned to see
Rose and all his unease about Burnt Island evapo-

rated. Alive, beautiful and real Rose. He would do anything for her, he thought. How foolish that made him seem. This overwhelming feeling of love. Lust was so much simpler, so much easier to trick, entrap and play games with. But *this*. These feelings for Rose. He felt them on the surface of his skin and in the heaviness of his heart. He had been transformed to lead because there was no answer to this.

He could see the outline of her breasts, her smell jasmine and animal at the same time. He felt his body pulled towards her. When he looked into her eyes, he felt he was looking into his own gaze reflected back at him and he had to look away.

'I hate how I'm so desperate for you,' he whispered to her as they walked back to the house.

She took his hand.

'And what is so wrong with that? I love desperate. Desperation is born of longing and need. Desperation is reaching for the moon. People who aren't desperate – there's something wrong with them. They're not thinking straight. We're all splashing around in the maelstrom whether we know it or not. Desperation is dark, it has weeds and ivy growing over it, it creeps through ruins. But show me someone who isn't desperate and I'll show you a fool.'

They went to bed. Rose seemed to enjoy and

embrace her complexity. And the uneasy wildness in her heart mimicked his. As he caressed her, he felt he could wear her away like the river did the stones, wear her away with his desire. Afterwards she looked drained and sullen and content all at the same time.

'How's the book going?' she asked.

He gave her the most forced and brilliant smile he could muster.

'I've almost finished the first draft!'

What a destructive lie. Destructive to whom – himself? Her? James? The platonic notion of truth?

While James was out, Max returned to James's study. He went up to James's desk and, picking up his notebook, opened it. To Max's surprise, James had scored out all the names of the inhabitants of Burnt Island with heavy ink lines. And now, next to the notebook on his desk, lay a pile of closely typed paper.

He eagerly picked up the first page. But the page was covered by the same word repeated over and over again – a name typed continuously as a solid piece of text with indentations and paragraphs and commas and full stops, as if the repetition of a single name could make up a story. He flicked through the pages. They were all made up of her name in remorseless type. Not Natalie's name. *Rose's.*

~

That night, Max decided to visit Rose's apartment in the basement of the house. Walking along the corridor outside her apartment, he spied a pinprick hole in the wall. He looked though it. Inside her bathroom, he could see Rose running a bath.

Only her top half was visible, and Max watched her take off her blouse to reveal her round, white breasts. She then slid slowly into the bath. He could now see the lower half of her body. Her legs had merged into a tail of overlapping scales, aquamarine in the yellow light. Her lower body was in the twisting convoluted shape of a serpent, writhing and twisting in the water as if with its own independent life. She was soaping her breasts, as if oblivious to the repellent monstrosity of her form below.

Max quickly withdrew from the hole. The conflicting reality of what he had seen and what he should have seen collided in a rape of imagery. He walked slowly back to his bedroom.

The copy of *Lifeblood* that Dr Macdonald had given him was lying on his bedside table. He picked it up. The first page read:

'She's volatile like the sea. She scares and arouses

*me in equal measure. Perhaps that's the point of
her. Of me. The sea had called out to her. She heard
the singing. I can hear it too.'*

He read further. *Lifeblood* was the exact replica of
The Song of Imagination by Daniel Levy. James had
plagiarised Daniel's novel in its entirety. Then added
an original ending to the unfinished manuscript. *Lifeblood* concluded with the two lovers, the woman and
the younger man, trapped in a cave. As the tide came
in, they had made love *'with the sea roaring outside and
a different roaring inside their heads'*.

The next day, Max came down to the living room to see
a letter for him, lying on the floor beneath the door. He
opened it up with trembling hands. It was from Luke.

Dear Dad,

*Please can I come and visit you? Mum is driving
me crazy. She keeps on rearranging my books in
chronological order.*

Love Luke.

Max took out his pen and wrote back.

Dear Luke,

Please, whatever you do, DON'T COME. This is a really weird place and wouldn't be a good place for a young man like you.

Love Dad

He posted his letter to Luke in the letterbox outside the post office. He had to stop Luke coming to Burnt Island.

Max saw the figure again dart behind the wall of the garden. He ran around the other side of the wall but he could see no one amongst the roses. He found it difficult to believe he could have mistaken a shadow for a figure; it was a late summer's morning and the garden was bathed in light. There was a sound of footsteps, the sight of a stooped figure (about his height?) moving across the lawn, unnaturally fast. But who was this haunting him? Was he an actor, a charlatan, a copyist? Who *was* he?

He looked out of the living room window over the dunes to the sea and it all seemed real but how could he be sure? The sense of space and light was giving him too much room to think; his imagination was spreading over the island like molten lava. He could pretend the island was still dormant, but his perceptions told him otherwise.

This place seemed full of deathly ideas. He began to start daydreaming about his own death. How would he take his own life? He could jump from the cliffs or swim far out to sea. And this dream of death became more and more attractive to him, a sinuous suggestion that wrapped around his mind like a snake. Suicide no longer seemed an act of insanity, but a sublime letting-go, a gilt-edged invitation to stop struggling.

The graphic nature of death, the specific injuries, didn't impinge on his imagination. Like a piece of unclear writing that he could edit, the gruesome details were extraneous, words that he could cross out and delete. The manifold drafts, the restructuring, the painful rewriting of sentences, could be consigned to oblivion. Max was concentrating on the stuff of the novel that made up its heart, focusing on the moment: the falling, the coldness of the water and then, with a sensitive edit, the leap to the ending.

Max struggled to start his new novel. *It was as if the strange events on the island were taking on the form of the horror he was trying to write.* If only he could channel his imagination back into his writing, he would be safe. But he could not. He was left looking down at his arid, yellow cards, full of neat back-story and character analysis.

He read again the list of his protagonist's sympathetic qualities. He gave him more conflict, lots of it, a new conflict mapped out in every chapter. He knew what publishers and agents and readers wanted was a thick coating of realism. But he didn't want to be a copier or a plagiarist of reality.

Later that evening, Max heard the sound of James's bedroom door opening. Max flung on his dressing gown and followed him down the stairs, his naked feet sticking to the slippery wood. He went from room to room, trying to find him, but James was nowhere to be found.

The screaming had begun again. The same ecstatic screams Max had heard over the previous weeks, coming from somewhere in the depths of the house. The cries seemed to be coming from an area below the kitchen. He entered the kitchen, switched on the light and looked around the empty room. There was the sink, the kitchen table and various cupboards. Everything looked just the same as it always did.

However, a door he had never noticed before, partially hidden by a small table, was slightly ajar. Moving the table aside, he pushed the door open. Steep, wooden steps led directly down into a dark basement. He climbed down and turned on the light switch at the bottom. He was now in a sparsely furnished room with a few storage boxes, an old sofa and a tattered rug on an expanse of concrete floor.

The only incongruous object in the room was a large, empty bookcase standing against one of the walls. Turning to go back up the steps, he switched off the light. But a chink of light still shone into the room. The light was coming from underneath the bookcase. Max walked over to the bookcase and, with the lightest of touches, it swung silently open.

The stone walls of the hidden room behind the bookcase were painted black and shackles were attached to the floors and walls. It was intensely claustrophobic, as if instead of walking into a room Max had walked into another's innermost private thoughts, thoughts of perverted desire. But these thoughts were real, they had been acted out, one by one, most deliberately. These thoughts had chains on them, had worn shackles and had cried out and bled with pleasure and pain.

Max was full of wonderment at people who actually acted out their desires. He had spent his whole life keeping his desires once removed either through fear or thwarted ambition. He put his desires into books or put his obsessional thoughts into dreams of his literary success.

A monstrous metal bed dominated the room with satanic imagery painted in lurid colours on the large embossed metal headboard. Pictures of contorted satyric figures sucked the blood from voluptuous, naked women but it was the real, naked woman on the bed that drew Max's attention.

Max couldn't see the young woman's face but could make out the hair – chestnut curls – and the gentle curve of her hips. A naked man was standing beside her with his back to the door, his grey hair falling loosely about his shoulders. Max quietly closed the bookcase behind him.

He returned to his room and lay down on the bed, looking up at the ceiling. Not only had James plagiarised Daniel's novel, he had plagiarised Natalie. *He had made Rose the erotic replica of his wife.*

The shapes of the furniture were outlined in the blackness. How objective the furniture looked, like empty gods. He thought of those who betrayed and the people who were left in the slipstream of their lies, not knowing what to do, what to believe, whether of the past, present or future. Liars travelled through time like time machines. Their lies fractured not only the past but the present and future: all tenses.

CHAPTER 19

THE SUBJECT, HE thought, was like one of his own novels. But it was not a novel he had written. Someone else had written it. He was stuck in someone else's book: James's book. And how he hated this book. It had not been well written. There was no symbolism in it, just the cliché of betrayal. *Or was it Rose's book?* Vulnerable, as she was, she must have been complicit in this fantasy of becoming a copy of her mother. *He had always known she was a writer.*

The shock of seeing Rose and James together was so visceral it had seemed unreal, every fibre of his being resisting the erotic nature of the information. He had moved sideways as the world outside remained outwardly the same. What was happening to him was the opposite of scientific; it was novel sensation. Everything he looked at was seen through the prism of their sexual betrayal. In the mirror, even the lines on his face had taken on a particular glow, the malevolent power of their actions having visibly aged him.

The only truth left to Max was his bitter, nauseous and merciless anger. James and Rose were a gravitational pull on his anger, drawing it towards them irreversibly. His anger needed them in order for him to survive. Without the sustenance of his anger he would be nothing. That was the truth.

He felt sick all the time now. His hands shook when he took up his pen to write. He looked at his diagrams and his little, yellow cards with the details of his characters written on them in such painstaking detail. And he realised how all his cards didn't add up to a hill of beans. His outline, his cliffhanger at the end of each chapter. What a charade. The devil had abandoned his writing, leaving it spiritless and lifeless, and was infiltrating his life instead.

His bestseller was stillborn. How could he breathe life into this tiny corpse of bones, limbs and hair? He threw the yellow cards up in the air and they flew up like two-dimensional birds, the sea blowing rough and stormy outside the window.

He started to write instinctively, without notes or cards or planning. Max found solace once again in the integrity of his imagination. His intrinsic creativity was his first true love, the first thing he turned to when feeling alone. It matched him, idea for idea, feeling for feeling, sometimes just beyond his ken. It challenged him in ways nothing else could.

His imagination was a shadow, an echo, an aspiration, a friend. His imagination took him down paths he had never known existed, made suggestions that at first seemed implausible, gave him feelings that he would understand only later. It was more powerful than he, more instinctive and brave. It was reckless and feckless and sometimes fey. And, unlike Max, was not interested in love or sentiment, just desire and feeling and words.

Pages and pages he covered in his almost illegible scrawl, about his arrival on Burnt Island, his love for Rose, his misguided friendship with James, their incestuous treachery like shifting sand. All related through the prism of his mind. He wondered if one day soon his imagination would possess him, would consume him in its darkness. And he would finally become at one with his longing.

And then, after the shock of their betrayal had subsided like the sea at low tide, Max was left with the detritus: the sea weed, the rocks, the shards of rotting wood. His feelings grew coldly angular, sticking out of the sand, conspicuous and unbreakable. Disbelief still coated everything he felt, similar to the wetness on the shore when the tide receded. His bitterness, like his anger before, became his lifeline; it kept him sane.

He couldn't – and this was the worst thing of all – forgive her. Forgiveness was beyond him as a bird reaches for a leaping fish, swooping and diving and missing, as the fish plunges swiftly into the depth of the sea, swifter then the flight of the bird, down into the turquoise-green sea until the water turns dark blue and then black, the silver of its scales enticingly disappearing into the darkness. So too was forgiveness, reconciliation – no matter how hard he tried – continually disappearing into darkness. He caught flashes of it glimmering, tantalisingly just out of reach.

It was all about perceptions of reality. What was reality but our perception of it to a matter of fine degrees? Now on the island the same things took on different meanings – reality looked the same, same Rose, same James, same island, but the significance of them had altered irretrievably. Everything had shifted to the left.

His beautiful, sweet Rose had become monstrous, strange, something other. A creature he no longer recognised. He was looking at the same face, which aroused the same feelings of love, yet knowing it held a different meaning. If not for the bitterness, this constant readjustment of reality would have driven him insane. But he'd always, of course, had problems with reality.

But he still desired her, still needed her. In bed, he told her he was starting to see monsters on the island, grotesque shapes. He did not say they were versions of her.

'Your fear is creating them,' she said.

'It's not. They're real.' He struggled to see her in focus.

'It's your imagination making them real.'

'You want me to stifle my imagination?'

'Yes.'

'I can't. It's like asking me to stop thinking or breathing.'

'It's your imagination that's slowly killing you. You're losing track of the real world. You don't know what's real and what's not. Your imagination is destroying you. Don't you see it?'

He stared at the face he had once loved to look at and watched it change into a demonic mask. He saw the green scales creep over her skin and her tongue transform into the forked shape of a snake's, flickering between her teeth. Her body moved sinuously and all her movements signified duplicity. And he desperately tried to rectify the situation, to transform her back into how he had seen her before, but he could not.

He turned off the light. But in the darkness, as he

made love to Rose, the arms that had been holding him tightly weakened and loosened their hold. Her nails viciously scratched his back, before her arms returned to grip him more tightly than she had ever done before.

He felt her chest, but instead of touching pliant breasts his fingers met the bones of a ribcage – her breasts had vanished. As he touched her rough and scaly skin, he could feel it leave a trace of dust on his fingers. Her skin was grating on him, scratching him roughly, her softness transformed to hard resilience, her flowery scent to an acrid, poisonous stench. Between her legs she was not warm and wet but dry.

'You are hurting, Rose,' he said.

It sounded ambiguous. But she simply sighed and held him so close that he could hardly breathe. He felt a cumulative sensation of pleasure at this consummate grip. The feeling of hardening metal. After her initial moans of pleasure, she had fallen silent. He became uneasy, not only at what was happening, but with the fear of what he would see if he turned on the light.

'Rose,' he whispered. There was no reply.

As he grappled with her new form, it was too late to stop the pleasure that had already started coursing through his blood. Like a stone falling down a well. He was now inside her, could feel her cunt coarsening around him like the crumpled paper of a discarded manuscript. Afterwards, he lay across her body, his semen drying and pricking his skin, spent and exhausted. His erotic pleasure diminishing as surely as the tide ebbs away.

He knew he had to turn on the light to face the truth. But before he had time, he heard a quick rustling of folding wings, and the bed lifted imperceptibly, as if a weight had abandoned it. He saw an outline of some reptilian creature slither out of the room. By the time Max had reached for the light and switched it on, the creature had gone. He was lying alone on the bed, a stain of semen on the rumpled sheets.

Seized by a feeling of utter fatigue, as a few moments earlier he had been gripped by pleasure, he fell into a dreamless sleep.

CHAPTER 20

POSSESSED, MAX WROTE chapter after chapter of his new novel, unable to stop, the words streaming out of him. He wrote down what he saw and felt, as if Burnt Island was now dictating to him what to write.

One day in his bedroom, as he manically covered the blank pages, he became overcome by an intense anxiety. Esther seemed to be crying out to him. This anxiety was made of shadows, fleeting images and thoughts. It was not specific enough to pin down like a butterfly with shiny turquoise wings displayed in a glass case. His anxiety was like a butterfly fluttering around his head, an all-seeing false eye on its dusty wing.

Wherever he walked or sat down, his anxiety would be fluttering around him. He could almost hear the sound of its fluttering wings. Flutter, flutter, *flutter*. His anxiety was making his hands shake, twisting his body into unnatural, twisted postures.

Help me.

The sound of Esther's words in his head was like a blast of white light in the form of letters. Accompanied by a loud noise: a bang of the single beat of a snare drum, hard and quick with a ringing reverberation. Had he imagined it? But the words had seemed so vehement, so external, so intrusive. He had felt almost violated.

But wasn't that part of madness – to hear your own voice and think it was someone else's? Writing, he thought, was on the first rung of the ladder to hearing voices. No, hearing her voice inside his head had been shocking but also natural and inevitable. More real and meant than if she had spoken the words out loud to him.

He had to find her. Now. As the wind howled and the rain lashed against his face, he rambled over the island shouting out her name. He finally found her on the east side of the island standing at the edge of the highest cliff, her arms motionless by her side. He could see her imagination, too, had become possessed by the island's thoughts and dreams. The sea crashed on the rocks far below, stormy and demanding.

'Esther,' he shouted out to her through the violent gusts.

He slowly approached her, step by cautious step. Looking at her standing alone, drenched in the rain and wind, he felt a profound intimacy with her, a feeling that they were physical extensions of each other. Her need and his need had become reflections of each other.

A drop of blood was seeping from her lips. And then to his shock another drop of blood appeared as if by magic. The back of her hand swept it away then another blossomed like a small red flower. Blood started to drip from her nose.

She couldn't express her emotions so she was bleeding them out drop by single drop.

She was looking at him dully, her skin pallid, her eyes glazed. The blood from her lips and nose continued in a remorseless flow. And then blood started to seep from the corner of her eyes. She was starting to cry blood. Dread crept over him like a cold hand. But just as suddenly as it had begun, the blood stopped flowing.

She slowly turned her head, as if an automaton, as if against her will. She walked right up to the edge of the cliff. Max felt an intense pressure in his chest, just imagining the drop below. In spite of himself, he was visualising the rocks, the ferocity of the sea, *the falling*.

She put out her hand to stop him coming nearer.

He was now only feet away from her. The rain was dripping down her face, her cheeks now reddened and roughened by the wind. She looked like a desperate, drowning creature. Her imagination had already left the world of dry land.

'Don't, Esther. Don't go any further. It'll be all right.'

His heart was pounding. He knew he had to keep calm. Had to seem real to her when the world was disintegrating around her. Keeping his eyes looking straight ahead so he didn't have to look down, he outstretched his hand.

She looked at him with her big, colourless eyes. All he could see now was a terrible acceptance in her eyes – not pain – but an acceptance of pain – and that this was what her life was necessarily about. Such knowledge. But, of course, Esther had always had knowledge.

That had been the problem since he had first come to the island: Esther's knowledge. It had always been an unspoken but undeniable fact that she had known everything. That she had known about the room, had seen her father and Rose together there. And that knowledge was what had silenced her. What had stopped up her mouth.

He looked at the mute girl. He felt powerless in the face of her powerlessness.

'Esther, you mustn't jump,' he shouted through the blinding rain. 'You're loved.'

She gave him a hard, disbelieving stare.

'Your father loves you.'

He doesn't.

He heard the words in his head, loud and clear.

He loves Rose.

At that point, she took a step nearer the edge of the cliff. It was wet, the grass slippery and long, and she lost her footing. She stumbled and fell towards the edge. Max threw himself forward, almost falling over the precipitous drop himself, and caught her as she tripped. He managed to stop himself going over the edge by hurling himself back, grasping her tightly in his arms.

They fell together safely, onto solid ground. He held Esther close to him as she lay shivering in his embrace, still silent, frighteningly silent, the wind blowing around them.

'*I* love you,' he whispered in her ear.

He carried her wet, cold body back to the house. The angst and bones of this young girl in his arms had become a cruel manifestation of all the secrets this family kept hidden under its respectable, successful veneer. Esther's muteness *did* matter. Was of consequence. It was emblematic of a secret so dark, it had led her here.

He could see through the lit window Rose preparing her supper. Her chestnut hair shining under the neon light. It looked like an idyllic scene. And he watched her face, her sublime, indifferent face, and suddenly felt he didn't know her at all. But of course he didn't; this wasn't Rose at all. It was her doppelgänger.

He carried Esther over the threshold.

The dread of the place became palpable. Slight noises, brief shadows, unexpected noises, all began to startle Max. He seemed to be living on the outer edge of his skin. The island, with its cypresses and dunes, had become malevolent. Burnt Island was changing from his place of escape and hope into a nightmare he could not escape from.

That night he dreamt he was sitting in his final therapy session with Dr Hoffman.

'Aristotle believed daemons invaded the melancholic

imagination,' she was explaining to him, 'gave it visions. Creativity is like little daemons coming into your imagination and playing havoc with your mind. Perhaps this island is the result of your creativity. You're creating the daemons around you.'

'No, I'm not. I'm sure the devil is on the island.'

'You don't think you may have created him?'

'What makes you so sure it's male?' He was feeling argumentative.

'You think it may be a woman? Of course, as a man, the devil you would have created would be female.'

'That's very sexist of you, Dr Hoffman.'

'Just stating a fact. The devil is woman etc.'

'I happen to love women.'

'Generically, perhaps. Not specifically. There is a difference.' She was laughing at him.

'All I know is that there is someone on this island causing this chaos. These monstrous events,' he insisted.

'It could be you.'

'No, impossible,' he said, outraged.

'And these events are the result of all your repressed emotion.'

'You know, James has all the charm of the devil,' he pointed out.

'It's too obvious.'

'It could be a double-bluff,' he insisted.

'What about Rose?' she asked.
'Well, she is female,' he said, sardonically.

CHAPTER 21

As Max ambled through the dunes, deep in thought,
an arm suddenly grasped him from behind. Startled,
he looked around. Standing before him, tousled and
handsome and amused, was Luke. Luke had the face
of an angel, with wide-apart blue eyes, a small nose
and a wide mouth. When Max looked at Luke he could
never quite believe in what he was seeing. Had he and
Dot really created him out of their DNA? He was more
like a vision of his imagination, he thought, a Blakean
figment.

'Luke, what are you doing here?'

'Your letters were getting more and more weird.'

'I told you expressly, I didn't want you to come.'

'Only because you've *never* had time for me. Not
properly.'

'Luke, it's not to do with that any more – it's for
your own safety.'

Luke was wearing his *Ghostbusters* T-shirt. *I'm not
afraid of no ghosts* was written on it.

'You're making the island sound like it's out to get
us.'

'It is.'

'I'm cold. Can I have a cup of tea?'

'You have to go home. It's too dangerous here.'

Max was growing angry. He was beginning to panic. He felt Luke was vulnerable here. Not only because of his age but because *he was his son*. If anything should happen to Luke, he would not be able to bear life any more. Luke had never demanded anything from him. Ever. But perhaps that wasn't the point. Perhaps, Max thought, he should have demanded more from himself. He wondered how he could get Luke home, what he had to do to persuade him to go home.

'I'm amazed your mother let you come here.'

'She didn't.'

'What do you mean?'

'She thinks I'm staying with one of my friends for a few days.'

'You don't think she'll find out? She has a nose for these things.'

'Nah.'

'Well, you're getting the ferry back tomorrow.'

'OK, Dad.'

'You're humouring me.'

'I'm not humouring you. I'll get the ferry tomorrow.'

'I don't believe you.'

'You're always trying to get rid of me. Run away from your family.'

'It was your mother who left me!'

'You know what I mean. Run away from us in your head. You were never with us really. Even when you were sitting with us on the sofa, watching telly.'

'Luke, writing was my career! It didn't mean I didn't love you. Didn't love Dot. You were both always in the back of my mind.'

'But that's not enough, is it, Dad? That's not where we belonged. In the back of your mind *while you were making things up*.'

Max looked at his son. All the pain and guilt for the loss of his family, all the regret for the sacrifices he had made for his writing, washed over him in a single, black wave. He looked at Luke starting to walk away. Max was in awe of the way his body moved so freely. No encumbrances, no failed dreams. To Max it was like he was flying. But the most wonderful thing of all about Luke was his guilelessness.

'Wait,' Max said. Luke stopped. *None of his novels had been worth a hair of his head.*

'You're right, Luke. It's not where you and Dot belonged.'

'So why don't you leave too? Come back home with me.'

'I can't.'

'Why not?'

Max looked into his open, clear eyes. 'Because it's too late.'

That night, James, Max and Luke ate a Spanish omelette that Max had cooked. As they talked Max could feel the difference that Luke was making to the dynamics of the house. Oddly, he was creating an atmosphere of hysteria. James was shining more brightly than ever, telling jokes and laughing at Luke's jokes, as if he were a child emperor. Luke was young enough to believe in it all, but Max felt suspicious. Then he thought, I am suspicious of everything at the moment *because I have to be*.

'Stay for as long as you like, Luke,' James was saying. 'Rose and Esther are away shopping on the mainland. You can stay in Rose's apartment.'

Max didn't say anything. James had mentioned Rose in a very casual way. James caught Max staring at him.

'Rose has finally finished with Ryan, Max. Such a relief. She finds it impossible to commit to anyone.'

Max sensed the malice behind James's smile.

'Luke's getting the early morning ferry tomorrow,' Max said, nonchalantly.

James smiled. 'What a pity.'

And James plied Max with Cognac. 'To celebrate the visitation of your first-born son.'

Max went up to his room. His desk was now covered in reams of paper: the handwritten draft of his new novel. It was almost finished. It was not the bestseller he had set out to write. It was a novel altogether stranger and more difficult: concentric, stories within stories of replicas and shadows. It seemed to be about the power of imagination itself. He was going to call it *Burnt Island*.

Max slept in and Luke missed the ferry. Stumbling out of bed, Max looked out of the window and saw James walking in the garden amongst the geometric hedges with Luke by his side. He was sure James was plotting something. He wasn't sure what, but he became frighteningly convinced Luke had become part of his story. He had to get Luke off this island. Quickly. He cursed himself for sleeping in and then remembered the cognac James had plied him with the night before.

Max had to act. He had to step out of his natural role of bystander and voyeur. He saw James walk down the garden, inclining his head towards Luke. What on earth could Luke be saying that interested James so much? He then watched, as James, advancing in the manner of a fond uncle, put his arm around the boy while they walked back towards the house, the window panes glistening in the sun.

Max caught hold of Luke's arm, that evening, alone in the corridor.

'What were you talking about with James?' he demanded.

'You're never normally interested in my conversations, Dad.'

'Well, I am this time.'

'Lots of things. Different things. He told me he's leaving the island to join his daughters on the mainland for a while. He must have already gone. We also talked about you.'

'Me?'

'Yes. He wanted to know more about you.'

'What did you tell him?'

'Just things. He says he has a lot of respect for you.'

Max felt flattered. His need for validation was a bottomless well. Max couldn't stop himself, *in spite of everything*. 'Oh, what did he say exactly?'

'That he's going to help you. Make your next novel succeed beyond your wildest dreams.'

'Did he say in what way?'

'In every way. *"Ways that Max can't even imagine."* Those were his exact words.'

Max thought of the almost completed manuscript of his new novel, *Burnt Island*, safely tucked away in one of the drawers of his desk. Perhaps with the endorsement of James his writing would finally find the recognition it deserved. But then he remembered he could not trust James any more, *not in any way*.

'Luke, it's dangerous here. *You have to get off the island.*'

'I've come to help you, Dad.'

'You can't help me. I have to deal with this on my own,' Max said.

Luke stormed upstairs to Max's room in a travesty of a teenage tantrum, except it wasn't about an untidy bedroom. All impulse and self-pity, the defining characteristics of his age.

Max looked around to see that a strange woman had suddenly appeared in the living room, sitting on the sofa. It was as if she had come from nowhere. He could only see the back of her head.

'Hello?' Max said carefully and the woman turned around. It was Dot.

'Dot! What are you doing here?'

She looked different. She looked ravaged. She looked the same but different.

'Is Luke here?'

'Yes.'

'Is he safe?'

'Yes.'

She had big bags under her eyes. Her skin was sagging. She was wearing a beanie hat that covered her hair. But she looked beautiful. How did she do that, he wondered? And as she spoke he could see, through the large windows, a black trace move over the dunes towards the house. He ran up to Dot and, grabbing her hand, pulled her to her feet.

'Get away from the window,' he said.

'Why?'

'Shadows,' he said. 'Shadows.'

'I don't see anything,' she said.

'That's because you haven't been here long enough.' But he wondered also if Dot's pragmatism was shielding her from seeing the monsters.

Luke was descending the stairs, having heard the commotion.

'Get under the table,' Max shouted at him.

Dot was staring at Max.

'Max,' she said, 'Max, you've lost your mind. You've got to come back home.' She was looking desperately around the glass house. 'Whose house is this, Max? What are you doing here? It looks like a place out of one of your novels. Unreal. In fact, the whole place looks unreal. Like it's a figment of your imagination.'

She went over to Luke and knelt down under the table next to him and put her arm around his trembling body.

Max looked around the glass house. He imagined smashing it. Throwing a stone through one of the large glass panes, breaking the glass so it spiralled and cracked into glorious, jagged pieces.

If only he could somehow tear up the fabric of the island itself – rip its surface to reveal the truth lurking behind the cypresses and the stone colonnades. He knew he had to break through the illusion to find out the truth, and that it would take an act of imaginative destruction to do so. That would be the only way to find out what lay behind the façade. He felt possessed by a searing urge to do this.

He barricaded his family into the glass house while the creatures of the sea, shadows of the depths, continued to flow over the dusty sand and sand dunes pricked with grass, towards the house. With the lights on, all he could see was the reflection of him and his family in the glass, the light and interior of the house, and their own ashen, scared faces.

'Get upstairs,' he said to Dot. 'Take Luke.' She looked at him, surprised by his assertive tone.

'Are you sure? What about the kitchen?'

'Dot. For once in your life would you, please, not argue with me?'

Dot muttered a few unintelligible words and began to drag Luke upstairs. But Max could see, in the way she moved, she was scared. He had never seen Dot scared before. But, then, there had been nothing in her old life to scare her.

CHAPTER 22

HE WATCHED, THROUGH the window, three of the creatures approach the house. In seductively abstract shapes, they seemed to be changing form as they neared. They appeared to be taking on the shapes of humans. Shapes he recognised: of a man, woman and child. Shock filled Max's mouth like the taste of blood. *It couldn't be, it wasn't possible.*

He stared at the three impostors of his family, hard. How could he tell the difference between their physical veneer and his own family? Their faces' expressions were more flat and emotionless than those of his real family. The impostors also walked more relentlessly, to a stricter rhythm, as if to an external will.

As the three creatures approached him, Max felt an initial reluctance to harm them. It would feel like murdering his own family. But hadn't he destroyed his family already, anyway? With his writing. Pulled his family apart, so it was just various severed limbs strewn about a suburban house. As Max looked into the eyes of these doppelgängers, he realised he was looking at the opposite of love – not hate, that was love's twin, but indifference: an absence of feeling.

Towards the end of his parents' marriage, Luke had clearly sensed the coldness that had taken hold of Max's heart. Luke, with the animal instinct of youth, had felt the invisible barrier that had risen between his parents, as high, precipitous and real as a cliff face. He hadn't been able to find a foothold or a crevice to place his small fingers anywhere in its surface. All he could do was look up at the sheer cliff face that had grown up between his parents and blocked out the light.

That was the trouble, Max thought, he'd never felt he'd had a choice. But looking at the catastrophic events on the island, remembering Luke and Dot upstairs, he realised that, of course, he had.

Max's doppelgänger family stood outside, staring at him through the huge plate-glass windows of the living room. For a moment Max felt he and his family were just *their* reflections in the glass. Then he remembered Dot and Luke were still upstairs. Luke's replica walked slowly towards the glass door and opened it. He had the same enigmatic smile on his face as Luke had when he was asking for something he knew his parents didn't want him to have. Luke's replica walked into the room and approached him. Max simply watched. How could he attack what looked like his own son? But it was what he had to do. To save his real family he had to attack these fictitious versions.

Luke's doppelgänger was now looking at Max in a way he could not resist, with an expression of childish adoration. The boy's eyes had grown moist. *He had to be wary.*

'Don't cry, Luke,' Max said, as he watched him come closer.

When the real Luke had cried real tears, Max had felt as if those tears had somehow been blaming him. As if in his previous life, *Max* had been the replica. But the tears of this Luke moved him in a new way. He came nearer. The boy seemed now to be personifying the emotional core of Luke, opening up feelings between father and son that had been shut down years ago. Luke was now standing right in front of him.

Max's breath grew quicker and shallower. The intensity of his emotion was unbearable, the mixture of urgent love for his son and Max's struggle to accept that this creature in front of him was not the Luke he knew. Suddenly the replica stiffened. A malign look entered its eyes and it leapt at Max with the full force of its weight and a latent, inhuman strength.

The desire to protect his real family gave Max unusual courage. He drew back his fist and with all his strength punched the imposter hard in the face, feeling its cheekbones crack beneath his hand. The doppelgänger's face contorted before returning to its original shape, as if Max had merely punched its reflection in water. Max hesitated, uncertain what to do next, and the imposter, sensing his doubt, lifted its leg and kicked him viciously in the stomach, sending him flying across the floor. The back of Max's head cracked hard against the wall.

Momentarily stunned, he could just make out, through blurred vision, the outline of the doppelgänger running towards him with unnatural speed. Unsteadily, Max rose to his feet and, bracing himself, took the full brunt of the collision. With all the inhuman strength of a man protecting his loved ones, Max tackled the doppelgänger to the floor, repeatedly kicking it in the head until the twisted, empty replica of his son lay motionless.

Immediately, Dot's replica walked through the open door. She had the real Dot's hard-cut, pretty face. Those blue eyes were like chipped glass. This replica had all Dot's resilient pragmatism. It looked identical to her. And then, the worst thing of all, it smiled at him with the young Dot's radiant smile. The smile, like the doppelgänger, seemed so real, but in his heart Max knew this was a fabrication. Simultaneously – he could not help it – his heart was stirred and a deep feeling for her was aroused, a love for the Dot he had married. A love, which, in spite of all the extreme vagaries of their marriage, had remained, unspoken, throughout.

But this doppelgänger was not the Dot he had loved, the mother of his child, even though it had her smile. His heart was racing. Racing at the pained audacity of the replica's existence.

The replica of Dot came towards him, reached out its hand. He hesitated, looking into its eyes.

'I can't take your hand,' he said. 'I no longer know who you are.'

'I'm Dot. Your wife.'

'No. You're not Dot.'

But even as he spoke, he wondered. Is it real, after all? Perhaps it is not a fake. He felt himself weakening. She wore the expression of the Dot he had fallen in love with when they had first met.

He took her hand. It was, to his surprise, hot. But too hot. Dot's hands were always cool. But it would be all right. As he looked into her eyes, it was as if she were dragging him into her gaze, making him fall in love with her all over again, compelling him to believe in her. And he could not fight her. She leant closely towards him so he could see the unnatural smooth-ness of her skin.

She was going to kiss him. As she put her warm

hand to his face, he felt a sense of doom. Her fingers scratched him lingeringly and deliberately down his face and then moved to poke him ferociously in both eyes.

Max managed to turn away and, as he did so, struck the replica hard across the chest with his elbow. As it fell, he pushed it backwards through the window, impaling it on a shard of broken glass protruding from the window frame. Its body twitched for a few moments before falling still.

Max ran up the stairs to where Luke and Dot were huddled by the bed. He bent down and hugged them tightly.

'You have to get to Peter Samson's,' he said, 'next to the garage. He'll help you.'

Dot looked at Max's hands, which were covered in blood.

'Max, it's *you* who needs help! Don't you see?'

'Don't argue with me.' He took them out by the back door so they wouldn't see the aftermath of the fighting and showed them the way to the village.

'You can catch the ferry in the morning,' he told them.

'But what about you, Max?'

'I'll be OK. I'll join you soon, I promise. When I finish my book I can leave. Now go.'

He watched Dot and Luke run over the dunes through the darkness in the direction of the village. They would be safe soon. That was all he wanted now, for his family to be safe.

He woke up on the living room floor, alone. Dot and Luke's doppelgängers and all traces of the fight had gone. The only evidence of the night before was the broken window, the cold wind blowing in through a large star-shaped hole. Through the hole, he could see his own doppelgänger waiting for him in the shadows of the cypress trees. This time, he knew what he had to do.

Leaving the house, Max walked slowly towards the figure, whose face was obscured by the shadows. He knew, just as it flicked its dark curly hair from its face, exactly what it would look like. His own face looked back at him – not petrified, just dully gripped by a devastating ennui.

Max opened his mouth but found himself unable to speak.

'I've come for you,' it said. 'It will soon be time.'

Max knew what it was talking about. Here on this island, his literary knowledge had actually become useful. He knew doppelgängers were presages of your own death.

'But why? What have I done?'

'Nothing. You don't have to do anything to die. Everyone knows that. You just have to wait.'

Max leapt at the doppelgänger, as if by eradicating it he could eradicate his own death. But like the other doppelgängers it was real to his touch, peculiarly fleshy and made of bone. Max punched it to the ground and, as it lay there, bent down and twisted its neck until he heard the bone crack. He then heaved it over his shoulder and dragged it through the garden, over the dunes and sand, into the sea. He watched it sink slowly into the depths.

Burnt Island was the source, the motif and the end. Max had been misguided to think that he could have come here to escape. The cypresses at the edge of the glass house, the beach of smooth gold sand, had all seemed out of a dream. How solipsistic, how narcissistic to think it had all been a dream. Such was his arrogance, he had thought he could shape the island. When, really, Burnt Island, in the end, had shaped him in its image. Its fiery embers, its petrified rock, its position in the middle of the sea had dictated everything that had happened to him, all along.

CHAPTER 23

MAX WAS NOW living alone in James's house. No one had returned from the mainland and he was enjoying his absolute isolation. His interior world now matched the exterior world seamlessly. He had reached the final pages of his novel. He would soon be able to leave.

As he took one of his long, reflective walks along the shore, he thought he could hear singing. It seemed to be coming from the sea. It was difficult to make out the melody over the roaring of the waves, crashing against the rocks that lined the shore. The waves were huge and loud but he was sure he could hear singing.

It was the sound of desire, the kind of longing that makes you want to cry, because, like life, desire is transient. The singing seemed melancholic and euphoric at the same time, as if the two were the same thing. It was not high pitched or low, it was like the murmurings of thought. He felt an over-whelming urge to enter the water, to walk into the depths of the sea, to follow the singing to its inevi-table end.

Just then, he heard someone call his name. He turned to see Rose walking towards him across the beach.

'Rose, you're back! You look so normal.'

She laughed. 'What did you think I would look like?'

'Did my family get off the island safely? I told them to go to Peter's.'

'They caught the ferry. Peter told me all about it. But he said your family were very worried about you. They didn't want to leave you. But Peter persuaded them it would probably be safer for them to go.'

She walked up to him and took his hand.

'I can hear singing,' he said.

She took his hand. She looked colourless.

'It's not singing you're hearing,' she said.

'What is it then?'

'It's just the sound of the wind blowing through the rocks.'

'It sounds like a Siren.'

'Women who lure men to their death? But I've warned you before, Max. Burnt Island is a place where your imagination can become real.'

Max felt a sudden surge of hope.

'So . . . You and James together . . . You're saying that was my imagination, too?'

But Rose looked down, unable to meet his eyes.

'My becoming her. *It was a way of bringing her back . . .*'

When her gaze finally met his, her grey eyes had grown dark to match the slate colour of the sea and her face was as pale as the seashell white of the sky. Her body had grown still, but her hair blew about her face like strands of seaweed.

'Rose?'

'Yes?'

'Do you ever get scared living here?'

'I'm scared all the time.'

'What do you mean?'

'Shouldn't we all be scared? Really. If we think about it. Scared that we're all going to die.'

He could only watch as she turned and walked away from him down the beach. That was the last time he saw her, her figure on the shimmering shoreline, walking away.

CHAPTER 24

THE SINGING WAS calling to him again, this time
not from the sea, but from the cave. He wanted to
track down the voice. It was the most enchanting
sound he had ever heard, as if emanating from his
deepest consciousness. It was a sublimation, everything he felt life was too black and white for. The tide
was coming in at a distance but he estimated he had
time to get in and out of the cave before the water
reached the entrance.

He entered the hollow of the cave. The cave's
entrance was large and, taking just a few steps inside,
he could see the interior of the cave with all its jagged
rocks piercing its sides and its towering perpendicular
structures. The sand beneath his feet was dense and
damp. The walls were covered in seaweed and lichen
stretching almost to the roof of the cave. It was like
being below the sea. He walked further into the cave.
The wall was glittering, as if encrusted with shards of
glass.

The atmosphere grew colder and damper as he
walked towards the back of the cave. Outside, the sea

was lapping gently up the beach, inch by inch. The singing was coming from the back of the cave. His heart was beating faster and he felt a rising excitement flow through his body, as if he were meeting someone whom he knew was going to become his lover for the first time.

The singing was fading away. He had almost reached the back of the cave when an anvil-shaped rock, lying just beneath the sand, tripped him up. A searing pain went through his ankle as he fell over onto the wet sand and he let out expletives through the excruciating pain.

He lay prone on the damp sand, trying to block out the agony that now radiated throughout his body. Slowly he managed to clamber to his feet, the pain making it difficult to think clearly. The singing had stopped completely as if his swearing or fall had frightened the Siren away. He looked back at the entrance of the cave. Water was beginning to lap there. If he were not careful, the tide would soon be filling up the cave. He started to hobble towards the entrance.

But his progress was slow and painful. By the time he reached the entrance, the water was flowing into the cave with a current that was too strong for him to keep his precarious balance. The current kept knocking him off his feet down into the sea. As he surfaced, the cold water had dulled the pain but reinforced his fear he was not going to be able to get out of the cave.

He flailed in the deepening water. Every time he struggled to his feet, the sea knocked him back down, engulfing him in its roaring, icy advance. Every time he struggled to his feet, the water had risen higher up his body. The seawater now reached his neck.

Just then, he spotted a wide ledge jutting out below the roof of the cave. Max managed, in spite of the pain from his ankle, to scramble slowly up to it. Exhausted and shivering, he lay on the hard, rocky ledge, as the sea lapped only inches below him. Max looked vacantly up at the cave's ceiling, only a couple of feet or so above his head.

Engraved into the rock were written the just-legible names, *Natalie* and *Daniel*, and a date: the day they disappeared. Max struggled to remember, through the pain and cold, the ending of *Lifeblood*. The ending James had added to Daniel's unfinished manuscript: the two lovers trapped in the cave by the tide. But how had James known what had happened to Daniel and Natalie? *How had he known what ending to write?*

Shaking with cold, he fell into a deep, hallucinatory sleep. When he woke to a sunrise, the tide had gone out. He was stranded on the ledge high up off the ground having lost all feeling in his lower body. He was feeling increasingly dissociated from reality. A figure was standing in the entrance of the cave, blocking out the light. It was James, his tousled hair on fire before the blazing sun, his features in darkness. He looked like Lucifer.

'James, help me,' Max cried out to him.

'You should have been more careful,' James replied, sadly. 'You should have left Rose alone.'

'Just as Daniel should have left Natalie alone?'

'I would never have suspected anything, but he left his manuscript lying out. *The Song of Imagination* told me everything I needed to know about them.'

'So you decided to follow them down to the cave?'

'Even though Daniel was losing his mind, it just seemed to make her love him more. He was pulled by the singing towards the cave and he took her with him.'

'And you just watched? You saw the tide coming in and did nothing?'

'You know the pain of jealousy, Max. Intimately. Natalie was mine. And you're not going to take her away from me, again.'

'Rose isn't Natalie.'

James gave a bitter smile. *'You're a good writer Max. I've always envied you.'*

Max fell asleep again and woke up to find himself alone, still lying on the ledge in the pitch darkness, the tide having come in again and the sea lapping around him. This time the tide was rising higher, over the ledge. The intense cold was making him feel tired and lethargic. It was like a sleeping sickness. Love sick, they called it, and he felt physically ill with impossible longing. Life seemed monotonous. His left shoe came off and he watched it float out of the cave into the open sea.

Snow reached to the edge of the beach and there was a strange sense of unreality as the snow on the land matched the white crests of the waves. It was lovely and yet it didn't make sense. The land and the sea sharing such identical whiteness. It felt vertiginous.

The snow formed little white static pine needles on the hard sand. Close up, it was not a blanket but crystals of snow, creating a network of lines through which the dark sand showed. Intricate, lace patterns of snow and darkness.

Snow fell deeply and thickly, turning the island to a blankness perforated by glass and dark trees and black wood. It had never looked more sinister and more beautiful than when it was all white. Max walked through the soft whiteness as if he were walking through the stuff of dreams. But here, in this strange uncaring, uncanny world, he had never felt he had belonged more. It was as if the island had become one of his dreams; he was dreaming the island and now he was walking through the landscape of his imagination.

But what did that make him? Part of the dream? He did feel oddly made up, an out-of-body experience, as he looked around at all that was exhilarating. He had a sensation of escaping from himself. He was someone different in his dreams. But this coldness, the terrible, terrible, deathly cold. *And there was the sound of the sea roaring inside his head.* The blue of the sky had the light green tinge that meant snow. The colours looked luminous against the rest of the black and white world.

EPILOGUE

A YEAR LATER in London, the cavernous Guildhall was thronging with the great and the good of the literary world. In the candlelight the ornately wrought orchids looked more like sculptures than plants.

The hall was full of the laughter and conversation of perceptive and well-read people. Perfumed women and tobacco-stained men vied to communicate what they knew to each other. The launch party of James Fairfax's second novel, *Burnt Island*, was one of the highlights of the publishing year.

He entered the hall with his daughter Rose on his arm. She was wearing a long red dress that shimmered as she moved, like rubies.

Marjorie Stone, editor of a financial magazine and an old friend of James's from his banking days, appeared by his side, as if by magic. She had the brittle, glamorous look of a mature French actress with crimson lips and dyed-blonde hair and a vivacity that refused to be dimmed by age.

'A marvellous novel, James. Absolutely compelling. You depict the descent of your hero into insanity with such authenticity. And this work is so different from *Lifeblood*. It's as if it's written by a completely different person – the style is so much more enigmatic.'

James nodded graciously as he noticed a glint come into her already knowing eyes.

'But I hear that you lost another lodger a while ago. Most careless of you,' she continued.

'Very unfortunate,' James replied.

'He was another novelist, wasn't he?'

'He was, but I don't think you would have heard of him. Max Long.'

Marjorie looked blank.

'He drowned. His shoe was washed up on the shore a few months ago. He was a very good writer, actually. Wrote seven novels. But he just didn't get that lucky break . . . Rose grew very fond of him, didn't you, dear?'

Rose looked for a moment wistful and then smiled, bravely.

'It sounds rather similar to the plot of *Burnt Island*!' Marjorie exclaimed, innocently.

James chuckled. 'It does. I don't know why I bother really. Truth is always stranger than fiction.'

And everyone in the literary firmament around him laughed, as Marjorie's blue eyes lingered on James a moment longer than was necessary.

ACKNOWLEDGEMENTS

THANKS TO JEN and Chris at Salt, Jenny Brown, Alan Gillis, Allyson Stack, Robert Alan Jamieson, Susan Sellers, Roseanne Peploe, Whitney McVeigh and Alan and Mary Thompson.

The quotation on p. 62 is from 'He Wishes For the Cloths of Heaven' by W.B. Yeats.